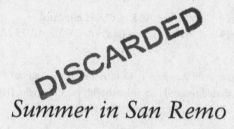

DISCARDED

Summer in San Remo

Evonne Wareham

Where heroes are like chocolate – irresistible!

Published 2018 by Choc Lit Limited
Penrose House, Crawley Drive, Camberley, Surrey GU15 2AB, UK
www.choc-lit.com

A CIP catalogue record for this book is available
from the British Library

ISBN: 978-1-78189-424-8

Printed and bound in Great Britain
by Clays Ltd, Elcograf S.p.A.

In loving memory
Bernice Elaine Wareham
1920–2015

Acknowledgements

Thank you to the team at Choc Lit for showing such
patience when it seemed that this book would never
see the light of day. And, of course, to the members
of the Tasting Panel who originally chose it: Heidi B,
Jan B, Hrund, Nicky S, Rosie F, Betty, Robyn K
and Sammi S. I'm sorry that it took so long!

Thanks to Simon for the suggestions about the
computer, to Kath of The Nut Press for the series'
title, and to my family and friends, particularly those
from the Romantic Novelists' Association and the
Wye Chapter of the Crime Writers' Association, for their
support and encouragement through difficult times.

This is traditionally the point where the author accepts
responsibility for any errors. So – all mistakes, improbable
plot twists and outrageous coincidences are mine.

Chapter One

Cassie Travers had handled a few unusual commissions in her time, but this one took the prize for the strangest.

She bounded up the last two steps, red hair flying, and threw open the door of her office with a flourish.

'I have to have a husband by tomorrow morning!'

Benita Wells, her best friend and sole employee, gave her a narrow-eyed look. 'Anyone's in particular?'

'I'm open to suggestions.'

Cassie bounced into a chair, green eyes glowing. She felt wonderful. The view from the window, of Bath's sloping streets of honey-coloured stone, was magical, even in the rain. Everything was wonderful. They had a new job. An *interesting* job. *There's even an outside chance we might make some money.*

Benita swivelled around to look her over. Cassie grinned. The grin was her secret weapon. She used it on clients, estate agents, car mechanics. If you could get the target to smile back, you were halfway home.

Unfortunately, it rarely worked on Benita.

Cassie knew what was coming. They'd been doing this routine ever since primary school. Bennie was the straight guy and voice of reason.

'You left here for a meeting – what, an hour ago?' Benita demanded. 'Now you're getting married? Did I miss something?' She rolled her eyes. 'Only you, Cass!'

'Stop making me sound like some sort of flake! We have a new client – Gerald Benson.'

'And?'

'He has a really simple job for us. All I have to do is fix myself up with a husband, by tomorrow.'

'That's simple?' Benita moved a file from one side of her desk to the other, with ominous calm. 'Look, I hate to break this to you, Cass, but I think it takes a little longer than twenty-four hours to arrange a wedding, even if you've got a man in mind. Which I know you haven't.'

'I might have.' Cassie pouted, swinging her legs.

Benita blew out a breath, ruffling her fringe. 'Honey, when there's a man in your life, the whole world knows about it. You sing. Under your breath. All the time!'

'I do?' Cassie stopped swinging, startled.

'Yes. It's a testament to the excellence of my temper that you still live. If you want to continue to do so, you'd better tell me what the hell you've got us into now, and why you need a husband to do it. What does this man Benson want us to source for him?'

'Nothing. Yeah, I know.' Cassie held up her hand. 'That's what the agency is supposed to do, but not this time. This is different.'

'Cassie – we don't *do* different. We agreed when we set the business up that we wouldn't take jobs that didn't fit the brief. We don't take just any old odd job. We're a *concierge* service.'

'A damn good one.'

Benita waved aside the interruption, refusing to be distracted. 'We source goods and services for people who don't have the resources or the time to do it for themselves. If this guy Benson doesn't want restaurant reservations, or a butler, or a new house, or tickets for the centre court at Wimbledon, he's not for us.'

'Yes, I know.' Cassie sighed. 'But that was before the not-so-petty cash went missing.' *Stolen. It was stolen.* Cassie scooped her hair away from her face. 'We're up against it, Bennie. Right now, a job is a job. *Any* job. This is strictly a one-off – Benson and his wife have been left a house by a reclusive uncle, who was very keen on the sanctity of marriage. There are conditions that have to be fulfilled, to prove that the Bensons are a loving couple and worthy of inheriting. It was Benson's childhood home. If he doesn't deliver, it goes to a distant cousin who wants to knock it down.' Cassie speeded up before the objection that was brewing on Benita's face made it out of her mouth. 'The problem is, Mrs Benson is into mountain climbing. Ten days ago she went off with her sister to climb Ben Nevis or something. Benson doesn't know where she is, and the first condition happens tomorrow.'

'So ...' Benita frowned. 'He wants us to find her?'

'No-ooo.' Cassie pursed her lips. This was the tricky bit. 'He ...' There was no easy way to do this. She plunged in headlong. 'Uh ... He wants me to *be* her. Just for tomorrow, to collect some papers. He wants me, and my husband, to pretend to be them, while he goes off to find the real Mrs B, and brings her back as soon as possible.'

'Well!' Benita exhaled loudly, opened her mouth, shut it, then opened it again. 'Cassie, that is the most outrageous load of bull I've ever heard in my life!'

'Yes, I thought so too,' Cassie agreed. 'I was about to walk out. *That* was when he mentioned the fee.'

She delved into her bag and produced a banker's draft, putting it down carefully on the desk.

Benita's eyes nearly fell out of her head when she read the amount.

'That's … that's …'

'Incredible,' Cassie helped her out. 'I know, but it's legitimate. I rang the bank. There are enough funds to cover it.'

'The cheque might be legitimate, but the job can't be.' Benita shook her head slowly. 'No one pays money like that for something so stupid. It has to be something else. Something big and nasty. Drugs, money laundering – or worse.'

'Yes. And I would *really* like to know what.'

'Hey! Come on! This is way beyond our pay grade. We shouldn't be touching it with a ten foot pole!'

'If we don't do it, someone else will.' Cassie tapped the cheque. 'This money is good. We need it. I propose we do the job, but we also try to find out what Benson is up to.'

'No way! You could get hurt. You could get arrested. You could get *me* arrested!'

Cassie puffed out her lower lip. 'I can take care of myself.'

Benita looked sceptical. 'Cassie, you do realise that doing this job involves helping someone commit fraud?'

Cassie pouted. 'Only a little, little bit.' She held her finger and thumb up, to illustrate just how little.

The set of Benita's mouth told her how much she wasn't convinced. 'Still fraud.'

Cassie's bravado collapsed abruptly. 'You think I don't know that?'

She cast a quick glance around the office. The premises were rented, the furniture and technology very definitely pre-loved, but everything here represented years of dreams, followed by months of hard work. Panic squeezed her heart. Now their successful enterprise was under threat from lack of funds. They had serious cash flow problems. And if they had to give it up ...

Could she still manage to carry on, somehow? Hold the business together using the old computer on the tiny kitchen table of her flat? She closed her eyes for a moment. If she *had* to ...

But what if this whole thing is genuine?

'If it was only about Benson inheriting some money, I wouldn't think of it.' She *really* hoped that was true. 'But this was his childhood home. Where he grew up. He's clearly loaded and willing to pay stupid money to keep it away from the nasty cousin. You didn't see him, Bennie. There were tears in his eyes when he spoke about the place.'

'So now you think he's for real?' Benita gave out a frustrated huff.

'I don't *know!*' Cassie didn't hide her own frustration. 'It all sounds mad, and suspicious as hell. But maybe, just maybe, it *is* real. Maybe that's *why* it's so mad. Tomorrow is only the first step. He'll be able to fulfil all the other conditions with the real Mrs B, if we can help him with this ...' She shifted in her chair. *Is it worth it?* 'I don't know why he picked us. But he did, and that might just save us from going under. And if it's not real, then it's something big, you said that yourself.'

A shiver ran along her spine and settled in her stomach.

Why had Benson selected them? It wasn't pleasant to think that someone believed she was desperate enough to bend the law, even if only in a small way. She'd always been scrupulously honest in her dealing with clients and the business community, and so far she'd managed to keep the full extent of their financial problems from common knowledge too.

Does someone suspect something?

With an effort she shook away the feeling of a shadow tiptoeing over her grave. 'If the thing is criminal. *More* criminal,' she amended, when she saw Benita's face. 'Then what we're doing is investigation. And we are *absolutely* the best people to do it. It's the only way to find out more about Benson. He's invited us into his scheme, after all. If we do the job and find out more, then we can take the whole thing to the authorities.' She sighed. 'We'll probably lose Benson's money, but maybe there will be a reward, or something.' She tilted her head inquiringly at Benita.

'Inspector Brown.' Benita said decisively. 'We tell *him*. He owes us one, after he sent us that woman who'd lost her Great Dane.'

The two women looked at each other and shuddered simultaneously.

'Good call,' Cassie approved, as soon as she'd recovered.

'Huh!' Benita aimed an accusing finger at Cassie. 'I vowed I'd never even *think* about that case again. It should have been a lesson to both of us. *That* was a job we should never have taken.'

'But the lady was very grateful when we found him. And she did stay and help clean up the office.'

'Yes, she did. And paid up promptly, with a bonus on top,' Benita admitted, laughing. Then her face sobered. 'Seriously, Cass, I think you should put that cheque from Benson in an envelope and send it straight back. Tell him we don't want his job or his money.'

'Mmm.' Cassie shook her head. 'The trouble is, we do.' The euphoria that had wafted her back from the meeting with Gerald Benson had all but evaporated. 'I know it's scary, but we do need this cash. We're going to have a hard time keeping the business afloat with what we make from finding hot tickets and collecting dry cleaning. What with the utility bills *and* next quarter's rent due.' She fingered the cheque. 'Look, let's just say that we consider it as a short-term loan until we get back in the black? We won't touch it unless we absolutely have to, but it will be there if we *really* need it.' She narrowed her eyes. 'Of course, absolutely the best thing would be to get our stolen funds back from that toad, Jason Fairbrook.'

Cassie's stomach was tying itself into a knot. It always did when she thought of Jason. Her hands itched too – to wrap themselves around his neck and squeeze. She'd given him her heart and the keys to the safe. He'd broken one and emptied the other.

She'd moped for three weeks.

Now all she wanted was to hunt down the good-looking, sexy cheat and get back what he'd stolen. She was working on it, between paying customers. He'd let slip once that his aunt had a place in the South of France that he visited often. *I am going to catch up with you, Fairbrook. And when I do ...*

'I know we have a cash flow problem, but this doesn't

7

feel right,' Benita persisted. 'We shouldn't be taking this money.'

Cassie dragged her mind away from her dismal taste in men. 'Look, sweetie, we both have some funny little habits, like needing to eat regularly. If we don't get cash soon, there's a real danger the firm will go belly up. In the grand scheme of things we don't need a vast sum to keep going, but you know the bank won't help.' Cassie ground her teeth. She'd provided every set of accounts, every projection, every bit of paper the bank manager had asked for, but the answer had still been no. As a small business, with few assets except their skills, they didn't have enough to offer in the way of security. They ran on a shoestring, but it was a *successful* shoestring. *Until Jason.*

He'd chosen his moment well. The weekend of their biggest, most prestigious event yet. She'd had no time to do more than wonder, in passing, why so many clients had chosen to settle their accounts in cash on that Friday, but she hadn't dwelt on it. She'd found out afterwards, of course. Jason had asked them to, offering substantial discounts as an incentive. Those missing payments, and the regular sums he'd managed to skim out of the current account, had left them with almost nothing. She'd taken justified pride in her business savvy and organisational skills, but she'd still been taken for a fool. The fee from that big event was keeping them going, day-to-day. And every week more enquiries were coming in, from recommendations and word of mouth. In a few months ... but she might not have a few months. Frustration simmered in her veins. She'd been so close to all her dreams, only to see them melting away. Because of a con artist.

But now …

She nodded at the cheque. 'If we have to, that cash is rent and wages and the whole damn thing.' She dropped her voice persuasively. 'Come on, Bennie. Let's go for it.'

She saw her friend hesitate. She knew what she was thinking. They'd both put too much into the agency to let it go without a fight. Benita took a very deep breath. 'All right.' She nodded. 'I must be mad.'

'Not so that you'd notice, and you're in good company.' Cassie rubbed her hands. 'To work. Got to get me a temporary husband. Ring Simon and—' She broke off when Benita shook her head.

'Simon is backpacking in Peru.'

'Since when?'

'He left yesterday.'

'Oh well – Michael then.'

'Still in traction.'

'Paul?'

'Last I heard he was helping the police with their enquiries.'

'I don't believe this! What are we going to do?'

There was a long, anguished pause.

At last Benita spoke, 'There's only one thing we can do.' She stirred the pencils in a pot on her desk, without looking up. Cassie watched her expectantly. 'You have to call in Kings,' Benita announced in a rush.

'Kings?' Cassie frowned. 'Wenceslas? Elvis? Kong?'

'Jake McQuire.'

'Ahhhhh!' Cassie sounded as if someone was pulling her toenails out with pincers. 'No way! I would rather give you my best cashmere sweater than associate with that man.'

'You only have the one cashmere sweater – and you shouldn't make threats you have no intention of keeping,' Benita warned. 'What have you got against Jake?'

'You have to ask?' Cassie glowered, her mouth a stubborn line.

'That was a long time ago. Get over it.'

'I have. But that does not mean I want to be in the same room with him. Or even the same city,' she added, muttering under her breath.

'You know Jake is back in town. You're bound to run into him eventually.'

'Not necessarily. But I'll deal with that when I have to.' Cassie shrugged when she saw Benita's disapproving expression. 'Look, I realise the guy is your husband's best friend from way back, but he and I – well, let's just say we don't get along any more, and leave it at that.' She ran her eyes around the room, seeking inspiration. 'There must be someone else. I know, ring the theatre and ask if they've got any actors going spare. There must be an understudy hanging about who'd be glad of the chance to earn a few extra quid.'

Benita was shaking her head again. 'Haven't you seen the posters? It's a one-woman show this week.'

'Oh.' Cassie hunched her shoulders. 'The temp agency?'

'This I have to hear.' Benita pushed the phone towards her.

'What?'

'You – explaining to Miss Potts why you want this guy.'

Cassie huffed in exasperation. Benita saw her chance and took it.

'Look – if you are going ahead with this crazy stunt, then you need someone who can handle themselves, in case it gets nasty. We have no idea what this man Benson might really be up to. If you're going to investigate a potential crime, you could use some professional backup. All the people from Kings are highly recommended.' Benita pointed her finger to stop Cassie breaking in. 'A detective agency gets asked to do all sorts of things. They are not going to think this is weird. Well, not *too* weird.'

Cassie's head went back, but Benita didn't waver. She just kept on with the stare.

'I suppose it would be one of the men from the agency, wouldn't it?' Cassie said, at last. 'Jake might not even get to know about it?'

'No reason he should. He's not there all the time.'

'I don't know why he's there at all,' Cassie said irritably. 'The guy is loaded. He has a huge business empire to run. He should be out there, captaining industry, laying waste the stock market, taking over companies and stripping their assets – when he's not dating supermodels and playing polo – or whatever else it is billionaires do.' She was warming to her theme. 'He should *not* be messing about with a detective agency!'

'It's his mother's agency. An old family business. She's been seriously ill and he's helping out. You know all that. Give the guy a break.'

'Excuse me? Jake McQuire is the last person to need any breaks. Didn't he inherit half the world a few years ago? From his father?'

There was a pause. Both women eyed one another.

'Oh, all right,' Cassie capitulated. 'Phone them and hire

someone.' She brightened. 'Maybe they'll send that cute blond guy who works out at the leisure centre.'

Benita grinned. 'I'll see what I can do.'

Cassie stretched and stood up. 'I'll be in my office, if anyone wants me.'

Chapter Two

Cassie put her feet up on her desk and stared at the ceiling. She was too restless to settle to work for the moment. Images of Jake McQuire floated in her mind. And she didn't like thinking about Jake McQuire. *Too many memories.*

Benita and Tony, Cassie and Jake. They'd been friends all through school, part of a much bigger gang, but their foursome had always been special. Everyone had expected them to pair off. Tony and Benita had.

That last glorious summer, in the weeks before Jake went on to university, anything seemed possible. Cassie had been seventeen and wildly in love.

Recollection brought a lump to her throat.

After years of absence, Trevor McQuire had swept back into his son's life. And everything changed. Trevor was a rich, ambitious man. He'd wanted the same for his son. Instead of university, Jake had gone to New York. Cassie hadn't seen him since.

Looking back, she knew it had all been for the best. Their love had been just a teenage thing. *It would never have lasted.*

From the safety of twelve years down the line, Cassie could be cool and mature about it. Which didn't mean she wanted to run into Jake again. So, he was back in town? So what?

Bath wasn't that big a city, but now they moved in very different circles. Cassie's experience of exclusive restaurants and society celebrations was strictly on behalf of her clients. She hadn't encountered Jake at any of the events she'd organised. If and when that happened she'd be too busy to worry about it. And she wouldn't be attending anything as a guest where he would be present. *Which is fine by me.*

Yanking herself out of the past, she put her feet to the floor and reviewed the files on her desk, calling up a spreadsheet on her computer. The agency's remit – sourcing goods and services – was pretty wide, everything from providing the maid and butler for a special dinner party to waiting at home all day for the gas man to call. *But not usually impersonating a client.*

Not something she'd ever choose to do in normal circumstances. But circumstances hadn't been normal since Jason disappeared with their money. Sticking rigidly to her scruples might mean the end of the agency.

Shaking her head, Cassie scanned the spreadsheet. Jenni and Claire, the two postgraduate students who supplemented their funds by delivery sitting and running errands, had everything covered for the rest of the week. Benita would take care of birthday and anniversary reminders, with appropriate shopping, and sort out the final arrangements for a book signing on Wednesday and a gallery opening on Thursday. Which left Cassie with the one-off jobs.

She opened the nearest file and closed it again. She was much too edgy to give her best to a project for kitting out a couple of holiday cottages. The next one was better – contacting old friends and extended family for a lady from Cardiff who was planning a surprise birthday party for her husband, and who didn't want to be caught making calls. Straightforward and methodical. Cassie pulled the phone towards her and dialled the first Price-Jones on her list.

Jake McQuire stood on the pavement in Walcot Street, staring at the pillar-box red door in front of him. The colour was so typical of the Cassie Travers he remembered that he almost laughed. The single word *Concierge* was etched on a glass fanlight over the door. A laminated card, pinned to a shiny red panel, gave the opening times of the office. What had he expected? Sober colours and a brass plate? That wasn't the Cassie he had known.

He looked up at the first-floor windows. Her office was up there. *She* was up there. She didn't want to see him. Benita had made that clear. But now there was a job she couldn't do alone.

He exhaled deeply. What he was about to do was crazy. On an insanity scale of one to ten, it probably hovered somewhere near eleven. He knew it, and he was going to do it anyway. It was too late to back out now. *The thing has already started.*

He stepped up and gave the door a shove. It opened easily. He put his foot on the stair, and began to climb.

Chapter Three

The sound of a small commotion in the outer office broke into Cassie's phone calls. She was on her feet, ready to greet a prospective client, when the door swung open.

'Hi, Slick. How you doing? I hear you're prepared to pay money to sleep with me.'

Cassie's chair creaked in protest as she dropped back into it. Her legs had gone to water. She had just enough presence of mind to stop her mouth gaping. The only sound that came out of her throat, when she tried to speak, was a low moan.

He looked … gorgeous. There was no other word for it. Dark hair, those incredible blue eyes, the mouth, the cheekbones, lightly tanned skin, wide shoulders. He was bigger, bulkier with muscle, under the expensive suit.

He was in her office.

'What the hell are you doing here, McQuire?'

This time she got her legs under control and stood up. He was shutting the door behind him, smiling at Benita as he closed it. That smile …

'Sorry, Slick? Is there a problem? Benita said you wanted to hire me. Something about needing a husband?'

'Not you! Someone from the agency.' The words came out sideways, through gritted teeth.

He was looking around the room, as if he was valuing it. 'Nice office.'

'It would look a lot better without you in it,' she muttered furiously as she caught her breath and unlocked her jaws. She was an adult. She was in control of her life. She could do this. 'I was expecting one of your employees.'

'Oh.' One eyebrow went up. She'd always envied the way he was able to do that. 'Communications glitch. I thought Benita understood. All my operatives are engaged at the moment. I'm the only one available. I haven't done much fieldwork lately, but as we're such old friends—'

'I wouldn't dream of putting you to that much inconvenience.' Cassie convinced her wobbly legs to take her around the desk, as far as the door. 'You must have a million things to do. Really, it's not important. Don't even think about it,' she insisted, shaking her head and holding up her hand. 'I can soon find someone else. Much better all round. Nice to see you, Jake. Sorry you've been troubled.'

Her fingers slipped on the door handle as she tried to grab it. She nearly jumped a foot in the air when Jake's hand closed over hers. 'Cassie.' Oh, that *voice*. It trickled into her ears; dark, warm, full of the sound of promises that the bastard was never going to keep. 'Let's talk about this, shall we? Benita was quite frank. There *is* no one else. We're both business people. I know our situation is – unusual – but I'm sure we can be professional about this.'

Cursing Benita and her big mouth, Cassie wriggled her fingers out from under Jake's. They were all still there, but they felt funny. Sort of boneless. She stuffed them into her pocket, where they couldn't get out.

'I'll have you know, I'm very professional,' she defended herself, eyes flashing. 'I've been running this firm for eighteen months. I have a reputation, respect—'

'Fine,' Jake cut in, smoothly. 'I suggest we sit down and do a deal, on a strictly professional level. Forget we have history together. This is work. You have a proposition, I'm interested. We figure something out and we both make money.'

Money.

Cassie's head jerked up. She might have known. Money was to McQuire what blood was to sharks. Just the scent of it in the water and he'd come circling. And, dammit, if either one of them was going to make any, she needed him.

'Of course,' he went on. 'If you have issues, because of the past—'

'Issues!' Cassie hissed. 'You left town, twelve years ago, without even a backward glance …' She sucked in a deep breath and pasted on a shark smile of her own. 'But as you said, that's history.' She gave an elaborate shrug and stifled the desire to bang her head against the wall. Or better still, Jake's head. Aware that he was watching her every move, she crossed the office, sank back into her chair and leaned nonchalantly on the desk.

'You're right, of course. We can help each other.' Oh, that cost her. Pain stabbed at her gut. *If I ever get the chance, McQuire will pay for this. And not in money. Blood would be good. Very good.*

Following her lead, Jake folded himself into her visitor's chair. Cassie sighed. He'd not lost an atom of the casual grace he'd had at nineteen. She still remembered that body …

Business, Cassie. Strictly business.

'Okay, Slick, what's the deal?'

Succinctly, Cassie outlined Mr Benson's proposition.

'And you believe him?' Jake asked as soon as she'd finished. Cut straight to the chase. She'd always admired his incisive mind.

She shrugged again. 'There might well be something else going on. Benson might be some sort of crook, which is why we need to be careful. But the man's money is good.' She curled her lip as she saw the light in Jake's eyes. That was the bit that pushed Jake's buttons.

'So ...' Jake exhaled. 'You and I, posing as man and wife, go to London, collect some papers and deliver them to Benson's flat. We don't have to meet formally with anyone, or sign anything?'

'No. It wouldn't work if we did, seeing as how we are *not* Mr and Mrs Benson.'

'Mmmm.' Jake studied the ceiling, clearly thinking.

Cassie studied his profile, her nerves twitching. *All you have to do is reach over the desk, grab him by that expensive designer tie and haul him close, to where his mouth is in kissing distance—*

Ahhh! She pulled herself upright, with a wrench that made her rock in her seat. She could feel colour mounting in her cheeks. Where had her imagination been taking her? She felt nothing for this man. She didn't want to touch him. Hadn't wanted to for years ...

Jake finished inspecting the ceiling and turned back to her, with something speculative in his eyes. She hoped the flush was dying down. *What were you thinking?*

'It all seems very simple – which probably means that it isn't. I daresay we can hack it.' He was gazing at her now, in a way that made the back of her neck feel hot. 'Um ... this husband-and-wife thing—'

'Yes?' She forced her voice to sound as crisp as possible. It wasn't easy.

'How realistically do you want to play it? Only I seem to remember—'

'Well don't.' She bounced in her seat. 'You said it yourself McQuire, this is a business deal. You get a fee.'

'Yeah, well, I wouldn't want to waste an opportunity. Have a little fun, and get paid for it.'

'I don't think so, thank you.' She glowered as he grinned.

'Can't blame a guy for trying.' The grin got wicked. 'And it's a lady's prerogative to change her mind.'

A swift flash of temper sparked through Cassie. She'd opened her mouth, to give him the benefit of it, when the irony struck her. She nearly laughed. He'd only offered her what she'd been wondering about, seconds before.

She pulled in a breath. She could do it. She could go to bed with him, and find out *exactly* how the lean, lithe body she remembered had matured into the hunk in front of her. She could show him what he'd missed; make him want her, then walk away. *Just like he did.*

Use him, abuse him and toss him aside.

The prospect glowed for a second, before reality hit. Who was she kidding? This man dated starlets and models. *Dream on, Cassie Travers.*

'Yes? No?' He was watching her closely, head tilted questioningly.

'No.' She shook her head for emphasis. 'Sorry to disappoint you, and tempting as the prospect is.' She arranged her face to show how little she was tempted. *Liar.* 'We do the job. Kings gets paid. That's all.'

'Ah, yes – the fee.' His eyes glinted as he settled more comfortably in the chair. He looked so damned at home in her office. 'I'm always happy to discuss money. But don't forget, if you change your mind, I'm all yours. Any time, day or night.'

'If it happens, you will be the first to know.' Cassie shifted a pile of files to the side of the desk, so she didn't have to look into his eyes. There was laughter in those blue depths, no question, but there was something else there as well. Something hot. She didn't want to think about it.

'As you said, this is a simple job,' she said briskly. 'I'm prepared to pay … three-hundred pounds, plus expenses. I take it that's acceptable, for a few hours' work?'

'It's broadly in line with our regular rates.'

'Good, then that's settled.'

'Er … no. I didn't say that,' he corrected blandly. 'On the surface it's simple, but who knows? You might need the services of Kings on a retainer. And that costs. Benson paid you up-front. I want half, Slick.'

'Half! No way! And stop calling me Slick!'

The name took her right back to when she was fifteen and her quick thinking had hauled the gang out of a sticky situation. It still gave her conscience a pang when she remembered it, but hey – it hadn't been *that* big a fire. The old sports' pavilion had been scheduled for demolition in any case. They'd just accidentally helped things along. And learned a lesson about the unpredictable nature of flame into the bargain. A sort of win-win situation, really. Jake had been the first to use the nickname.

'It's a compliment,' he pointed out now. 'Cassie Travers, slick and smart as paint. Always was, always will be.'

'Huh!' Cassie dealt ruthlessly with a treacherous glow that had sprung up, mysteriously, in her chest. 'I've moved on since then. I'm all grown up now.'

'Mmm, yeah.' He gave her an appreciative top-to-toe glance. 'I'd noticed.'

'Get your mind above the belt, McQuire. We're negotiating here.'

'*You're* negotiating. I'm stating terms. Half. Of course ...' He paused.

'Yes?' Cassie bent forward, hopefully. She should have known better, when she saw the way he was smiling.

'If you wanted to reconsider the husband-and-wife thing, then naturally I'd have to think about what I was charging ...'

'McQuire! I cannot believe you said that! You think I'm going to sleep with you, just to save money? That is outrageous, disgusting, perverted—'

'Only if you want it to be, babe.' He leaned forward, eyes alight. 'What did you have in mind? Black leather? Masks? Handcuffs?'

A flush of intense heat surged though Cassie's body. Heat that sent prickles of awareness into the most sensitive parts of her skin. *Do* not *go* there. 'Right, that's it! Out! Out of my office, now!'

'Fine.' He held up his hands in a gesture of surrender, uncoiling from the chair. 'I'll go. I never argue with a lady. If you have second thoughts, you know where to call.'

He was on his way to the door.

Cassie said something extremely rude under her breath. She hated this, she *really* did, but she didn't have any choice. It was McQuire or nothing.

'All right.'

'What was that?' He slanted his head, listening.

'I said *all right*,' she repeated, goaded. Her tongue was almost curled with the effort of speech. She cleared her throat. 'Come back, please, and we'll talk – about money,' she added hastily.

He stayed at the door for a moment. Savouring his victory? Cassie was sure he could see all her mixed emotions clearly in her face. He looked as if he was biting down on another grin. He sauntered back to the chair and sat.

'Well, Sli— Cassie. Are we on, or not?'

'Jake ...' Using every ounce of willpower, Cassie summoned up her widest smile.

Jake sat up straight in the chair. He looked surprised, as if something had happened that he hadn't expected. Cassie blinked, disconcerted by the strange expression in his eyes. She'd finally caught him unawares. *How?*

With an effort she pulled herself back on track. She had to use whatever she could to salvage this. 'Look, I know you were joking just now, about us sleeping together. I ... overreacted. But the fact is, you don't need cash. You have shed loads of the stuff. If you could just see your way to—'

'Sweetheart,' he interrupted. 'I'd love to let you have me for free, believe me.'

Whatever it was that had taken him by surprise, it had passed. She knew her eyes flickered, betraying her annoyance. She was the one on the back foot here. All *he* had to do was stay cool and keep chalking up the points on his side. He was still talking, 'I have obligations, and the agency has overheads. I want half.'

'I ...' She took a breath, to give herself time to re-group. Now *she* had to be the cool one. She leaned back and steepled her fingers, trying to look like a woman wrestling with a hard decision. If she could pull this off ...

'Okay, I admit it. I need you.' Yes! She'd got the necessary words past her teeth, and the roof hadn't fallen in. Her nose hadn't even grown. 'I agree. You help me and I'll pay you—' She hesitated, showing reluctance. '—five-hundred pounds.'

'That's not half – it's not even close.'

'How did you ...' Cassie recoiled, realising too late what she'd done. She'd given away her hand, but someone else had a part in it. A big part. 'Benita Wells is going to die!'

'Did Benita know it was meant to be a big secret?'

'Um ...' Cassie squirmed. 'Well ... no.' She had to admit it. 'I suppose not.'

Jake gave her a measuring look. 'You have a job here that you can't do alone. I am willing to help.' He leaned forward. 'Now is a good time to make a deal, Cass.'

'There's never a good time to make a deal with the forces of evil! And that's where you belong, McQuire, no question.' She stabbed a finger at him.

'Bloated capitalists, you mean?' There was just the hint of a smile. He leaned a fraction closer. 'So —why not live on the edge a little?' His voice had gone soft, persuasive. 'Come over to the dark side.'

Cassie gave him a glare calculated to make a grown man shudder, then weep. It bounced off with no visible effect.

She was going to have to do this.

With a last pang of regret, she caved in.

'All right. You win. Partners. Fifty-fifty. Shake?' Without

thinking, she stood up and held out her hand. Jake rose and took it.

It was too late to draw back, to wish that she'd had more sense.

His fingers were warm and firm, with an intriguing hint of roughness. She swallowed, hard. McQuire had never been the manicure type. *And isn't that part of the problem?*

She had to forget all that, like right now.

'Partners.' He nodded as he let her go. 'I'll tell my people to talk to your people. Person. Benita. We have a proper contract, or the deal is off,' he warned.

'Naturally.' She faked nonchalance. Bugger. He'd thought of every angle. Not even the tiniest bit of wiggle room. She wasn't in the habit of reneging on deals, but the chance to be a little ... creative ... would have been nice. *All's fair in love, war and dealing with Jake McQuire.*

'I'll get someone on to it straight away,' he promised. 'After that, I'm entirely at your disposal.'

'Yes, that's what I'm afraid of,' she muttered as he turned towards the door.

His hand was on the doorknob when she remembered. In the cut and thrust of wrangling with Jake, it had gone right out of her mind. Would it make any difference? Surely Jake would have realised? But she still had to say it. 'Um ... the job ... tomorrow. Er ... technically it involves us in a fraud.'

'Sailing close to the wind,' Jake agreed. 'But necessary, if we want to find out whether Benson *is* crooked. If we hit on evidence of illegal activity, I can see that it gets into the right hands.'

Cassie didn't quite like the spurt of relief that Jake could take care of things. But if it would smooth the way ... Presumably detective agencies had channels not available to the general public. 'Fine. Cool. I'll see you tomorrow then.'

'That you will.' Jake agreed, grinning.

With a brief nod to Benita, who was on the phone, Jake strode across the outer office. Once on the other side of the door he leaned back against it, closing his eyes. Shock rippled through him. Hell – he'd forgotten what a stunner Cassie Travers was. And that smile! She'd looked up, right in the middle of arguing with him, and there it was. *Assault with a deadly weapon*. Totally unexpected, it had rocked into him, hitting dead centre of his chest. He'd felt it, right down to his toes. He'd almost lost the thread for a couple of beats.

Maybe this thing is going to be more of a challenge than you thought.

Well, bring it on.

The cute kid he'd known had matured into one heck of a woman. She was lovely, and then some – spiky, sassy, sexy as all get out. The red hair he remembered, green eyes, legs and figure to stop traffic – but he'd forgotten how smart that luscious mouth was in dishing out backchat. Cassie Travers took no prisoners. He wasn't quite clear *why* she'd decided he was the next thing to Satan's second cousin, but unpredictability had always been part of her charm. If he got through this without major damage to his pride and his ego, not to mention his wallet, it was going to be a miracle.

He peeled himself away from the door, running a hand

through his hair, a reluctant grin on his face. 'Deal with it, McQuire,' he told himself softly. 'You were the sucker who got yourself into this.'

The grin widened. Maybe things wouldn't shape up the way he'd planned them – but he could always fix that later. He swung onto the stairs, whistling.

However it all went down, working with Cassie was never going to be boring.

Chapter Four

Cassie knitted her fingers together and stretched her arms above her head, wriggling her neck to work out the kinks. A quick squint at the clock had her blinking. 7.30? Where had the time gone? As if on cue, her stomach rumbled.

Food and sleep. You have an early start in the morning.

'Don't remind me!' She looked round guiltily, when she realised she'd said it out loud. The office was empty. The whole building was probably empty. *No one to hear you curse. Even if the thought of tomorrow makes you want to.* Cassie wrinkled her nose. London – fine. With Jake – not so fine.

She reached out to close down her computer, taking one last look at the screen. The research she'd been doing for the last hour was for herself, not for a client. An idea she'd been meaning to follow up for a while. *And nothing to do with trying to prove something to Mr McQuire?* She shrugged. It was nothing to do with Jake. Why should *his* arrival prompt her to make a serious attempt at tracing the errant Jason? And the digging she'd done had been worth it.

She noted the names on her list, with satisfaction, before sending it to print and closing the files. It was a short list, but one that might pay dividends – the names of private gardens on the Riviera that sometimes opened their gates to the public. Jason had once mentioned that his aunt was a keen gardener, very proud of her large garden and collections of rare plants. If she was proud of it, there seemed a good chance she might want to show it off. None of the owners' names meant anything to Cassie, but a few quick calls in the morning might yield some information she could follow up. *If not, you'll just have to take a trip to the Riviera yourself.*

'Oh, yeah, fat chance. I'd be lucky to afford a trip to Bognor!'

Damn, she was talking to thin air again!

Anyway, in the morning ... Cassie groaned, in the act of reaching for her 'To do' list. In the morning she'd be miles away from the office. With Jake. Jake and Jason. Two bad apples in a pod. Or did she mean barrel?

Her stomach gave a flutter that had nothing to do with hunger.

She flipped the printout from the machine and switched it off. The trip to London tomorrow would take up most of her day. Just to deliver a package. *Tell me again – why are you doing this?* Cassie leaned back in her chair, muscles suddenly tense. The job was distinctly iffy, whichever way you looked at it. She knew that – had from the beginning.

So – why?

She chewed her lower lip. Even if the job was genuine, and she was saving Benson's childhood home from the bulldozers, she was skating on thin ice. If Benson hadn't made it clear that the collection of the package tomorrow was only a very small part of the conditions he and his wife had to meet, to protect their inheritance, she wouldn't have considered it. *Even for that astonishing amount of money? That you now have to share with Jake?*

Cassie chewed her lip harder at the memory of Jake, sprawled so confidently in her visitor's chair. *That* chair.

29

She glared at it. Promising him half the money rather messed up the idea that she would try not to touch Benson's fee.

Hmm. The money was a matter for another day, and negotiation with McQuire. *Now* she had to concentrate on getting through tomorrow. She'd committed to the client and the job, and she would carry it through. *But what exactly is the job? Do you* really *believe Benson's story?*

Cassie smoothed her finger along the arm of her chair. That was actually the point – in her heart of hearts, despite Benson's tears, she didn't. And if something else was going on, she and Jake were right in the middle of it. Which meant she had to do everything she could to find out what *it* was. Self-preservation, gathering information on a possible crime – and, she had to admit – rampant curiosity. Three good motives for keeping her wits about her and her eyes open tomorrow.

Cassie sighed. She'd been *way* too impulsive when she agreed to this crazy assignment. She'd let excitement and the thought of the money cloud her judgement. Benson had probably counted on that. All she could do now was press on, and learn from the experience. At least tomorrow would be the end of her enforced association with Jake. That was one bright spot to look forward to. She wouldn't need him around any more. He would be going back to the States soon. Then she could investigate Benson without any unwanted distractions. Whatever she found out, she could take it to the authorities herself. She really didn't need any more help from Jake.

Cassie Travers, ace detective!

Stuffing the list of Riviera gardens into a file marked

'Fairbrook' and dropping it into her desk drawer, she set about retrieving her possessions from around her desk – jacket, shoes – she had to feel under the pedestal to locate the left one, cramming it on as her stomach rumbled again, even louder. There was nothing in the fridge at home. She'd have to stop at the shop on her way. Get a ready meal, or something. *A ready meal for one. How sad is that?*

'It's not sad. It's convenient.' Cassie stood up, then hesitated, stalled on her way to the door by a sudden wave of uncertainty, and a quick, brutal stab of loneliness. She had masses of friends, including some of her clients. She could ring any one of them this minute, and get an invitation to supper in a heartbeat. *But friends aren't family. Or one special person …*

'Oh for heaven's sake! You're not *that* needy!' Even so, her hand hovered over the phone. It was a while since she'd called her parents. She couldn't remember exactly when. Maybe last month?

Somewhere outside a clock struck the hour. At this time of the evening her parents would be out, having drinks and tapas with friends. Or they could be entertaining golfing buddies with cocktails at home, before a late dinner. *Not a good time.* Making a mental note to try at the weekend, Cassie shouldered her bag. Calls to Spain were probably cheaper then, anyway.

She stepped out into the corridor and secured the door behind her. Maybe she'd forget the ready meal and stop at the chippy instead.

Jake stared out over the dark expanse of water. The breeze,

whispering through the open windows of the car, held a tang of salt. Lights from shipping in the Channel flickered, breaking up the twilight. Ma was out there, somewhere. *Crossing the Bay of Biscay? Or already anchored off some sunshine island, getting ready for a show, or dancing on deck, or whatever other entertainment the cruise ship provided?* He'd have to check on the schedule she'd left. She'd be visiting lots of amazing places. *Which is good. She deserves it.*

Jake frowned. She didn't need to go alone though. They could have spent some quality time together, just hanging out. But she'd been adamant about it.

He stirred uncomfortably in his seat, a lump gathering in his throat. He swallowed hard. When Ma first mentioned she was having medical tests, it hadn't sunk in. She'd made it sound like routine stuff. Even when she'd phoned in the middle of the day, to tell him she was having surgery ... It had taken a call from Tony, his oldest friend, to spell it out. His mother could be dying. It had hit him like a rock between the eyes. What a miserable excuse for a son he had been. The lump in his throat rose again. Once he knew how necessary it was, it had proved remarkably easy to drop everything and just walk away. On the way over, on the plane, all he'd been able to think of was the gift she'd given him – of a wonderful childhood: the Christmas treats, birthdays, holidays by the sea – all playing in his mind like a continuous film loop.

And in there too, in the background, in scratchy, jerky black and white, were Benita and Tony ... and Cassie.

He'd got to his mother's bedside right before the operation was scheduled. Had just had time to tell her he loved her, before they wheeled her away. And he'd been there, holding her hand, when she woke. He'd vowed then ... Whatever she wanted ...

He'd been a bad son. He knew that. Sitting beside his mother's bed in the hospital waiting for her to wake up after the surgery ... *What the hell were you thinking, staying in New York all those years?* He lifted his hand to rub the corner of his eye. Having come close to losing her, he really hadn't wanted to let her go away alone, even on a luxury cruise, but he hadn't wanted to deny her anything either. And then there was all the other stuff ...

The whole thing was weird, but he had a chance now to make amends. He'd work it out.

The breeze blew suddenly sharper. With a slight shiver, Jake raised the window a fraction. He wasn't all that sure *why* he'd driven out here to the sea. Childhood memories of time spent on the beach below where he was parked? Sandcastles and wave jumping and picnics with Ma – those long days of childhood that always seemed to be full of sunshine?

Hmm. Getting maudlin here. He looked at his watch. It would be after midnight when he got back and then he and Cassie would be off to London.

Cassie ...

He let out a long sigh. It was good to be seeing her again. Sure, for some reason she didn't think so, but he'd win her over. Would Ma approve of him helping her out? He thought she would. Maybe not some of the other stuff, but hooking up with Cassie ...

He tapped a finger on the steering wheel. Cassie was ... great. A hard worker, *real* good at her job – but her heart was too big. For a business woman, she was too trusting. That dirt-bag Jason …

When Tony had told him what that shite had done to Cassie and to the business – all but wrecking what she and Benita had worked so hard to build …

Benita hadn't said much, but he'd gotten the story out of a still indignant Tony – and found out everything he needed to know about the firm, over a few beers. Well, more than a few. And a couple of whisky chasers. He and Tone had been in complete agreement – those women *needed* someone looking out for them. And Jake was stepping up to the plate. He wasn't too sure about how much Tony would remember about all that. He wasn't entirely sure how much *he* remembered, but Tone was still speaking to him, so he'd not crossed any lines. It hadn't been too much of a stretch to plant the idea in Benita's mind that she was always welcome to call on Kings for help, now that he was back. Should the need arise. And with all Cassie's usual male helpers out of action … And a job that needed a man to complete …Well, stepping up to the plate. Almost a public duty. Spending time with a gorgeous woman and keeping the dirt-bags away. Just about perfect. The Benson thing … He grinned. Cassie *needed* him.

Hmm. She needs the Benson money. Which you are making her split with you. Yeah – but there would still be enough left to save her business. He'd made sure of that. No woman, least of all Cassie, wanted to feel like a charity case. Their agreement had to look good. And how could he resist going head to head with Cass over the negotiations when she looked so darn cute when she was mad? She needed the money, but she needed *him* to get the money.

An unexpected chill ran down his back. He cranked the window all the way shut. *Any man would want to be needed, right?*

Shrugging his shoulders to shake off the chill, he reached out to start the engine.

Of course, once you've delivered the package, Cassie will expect the job to be over.

Hah! No way!

Now he'd seen Cassie again, he was planning to go right on seeing her. Which meant that whatever happened tomorrow, the Benson thing *wasn't* going to come to an end. That whole inheritance story was enough to make anyone suspicious, let alone someone as curious about her fellow human beings as Cassie. She was a people person. She liked to know what made them tick, which was probably one of the reasons she was good at what she did.

Jake smiled. That was the key. Cassie would be curious about what might lie behind their unusual assignment. With the right kind of encouragement, she'd be ready to investigate.

And, of course, you'll be right at her side while she does.

'Perfect.' The car engine purred into life. 'Let the good times roll!'

Chapter Five

'Put them on, Slick'

'I can't.' Cassie looked down in horror at the rings nestling in the palm of Jake's hand. Two rings. A slim simple wedding band, and one that threatened to take her breath away. The delicate cluster of rubies and diamonds winked fire at her. Her hands were damp and her mouth dry, just looking at it. She couldn't let Jake put *that* on her finger.

'If we're supposed to be married, then you need a ring.'

'I know! But I only need something plain. I was going to stop at that place on the hill – the one that has all the cheap second hand stuff.'

'They won't be open for hours.' He'd captured her hand and was slipping the rings on. 'Stop wriggling!' He gripped her wrist to hold her still. 'I'm not planning to steal one of your fingers.'

'I don't like being manhandled. And I can't wear a ring like that. It must be an heirloom or something.'

'Heirloom?' The dark amusement in his voice curdled her knees, even more than the warmth of his fingers on her skin. 'It's not an heirloom, Cass.'

'Oh.' She looked down at the ring. It sparked and glittered on her hand. 'You mean it's not real?'

'They do wonderful things with synthetics these days,' he responded, looking bored. 'Have you remembered the directions?'

'Of course I have!' Cassie's hackles rose immediately. 'It's a place in the City, near St Paul's. Then Transford Mansions – that's in Chelsea.' She held out a battered A-Z of London. 'I looked it up.' She nodded to the other side of the road. 'My car is over there.'

'And mine is right here.' He began herding her towards it. 'Get in, Cassie, and don't argue.'

'Bossy swine.' The sight of the sleek Bentley convertible, waiting by the kerb, took the sting out of her quick flicker of anger. Who wanted to fight when she was being offered a ride in something like that? 'I suppose you're too grand to be seen dead in my car.'

'Dead is the right word. What's holding it together? Rust and rubber bands?'

'Archie has character.' She defended her beloved heap with dignity, glaring when Jake snorted with laughter.

'I might have known it would have a *name*.' He held open the door for her. She slipped into the passenger seat, inhaling the smell of expensive leather. She'd have to make it up to Archie later for her infidelity.

She had her seat belt fastened and the A-Z open on her lap by the time Jake slid behind the wheel. But of course she wouldn't need the map. Not in this car, with a satnav lurking amongst the controls and gadgets. She closed the book and dropped it into her handbag.

'Ready?' Jake glanced across at her.

'Ready,' she confirmed.

He started the engine. 'Okay partner. Let's do it!'

She kept silent as Jake navigated out of the city, luxuriating in the comfort of the upholstery and the smoothness of the ride. The sun was shining and the stone of the buildings glowed like warm honey. She felt good, even though her stomach was churning a little, with a mix of nerves and anticipation. She'd slept surprisingly well for a woman who'd done a deal with the devil.

She glanced over at the devil in question. His hands moved confidently on the wheel, and he was relaxed in his seat, easy with the big car. She looked away sharply. Watching him was sending too much warmth over her skin.

'I don't know why you were rude about Archie.' They were gliding into the fast lane of the motorway. 'The last time I was in a car with you, I could see the road through the holes in the floor. Oh – and wasn't the boot tied down with rope?'

'The ancient rust bucket I bought from Tony's cousin, when Ma was up north on a job.' Jake identified it immediately. 'It wasn't that bad.' He slanted a sideways glance at Cassie, grinning. 'I have very fond memories of that car. Particularly the back seat.'

'Yes ... well.' Cassie looked out of the window. 'I remember the way your mother yelled when she found out what you'd been driving around in. I was sorry to hear about her illness, by the way.'

'Thank you.' The softness of his voice pulled her head round. The grin had faded from his face.

Cassie experienced an irrational impulse to reach over and touch him, to express her sympathy. She shook it off. 'Benita said she's made a good recovery?'

'Yes – fighting fit again, or so she tells me.'

Cassie clutched gratefully at the idea. 'If she's better now, then I suppose you'll be returning to the States soon?' she asked brightly.

'Not for a while.' The grin was back. For some reason Cassie found the corner of her own mouth trying to turn up. She controlled it ruthlessly. This was no time for smiling – Jake was *staying*?

'Oh?' She dredged up cool unconcern.

'I thought Bennie would have told you—' He took his eyes off the road for a moment, to look at her. 'Ma decided she needed a holiday – recuperation.' The expression on his face now was self-mocking – almost as if he was inviting her to join in the joke. *What joke?* 'She's gone on a world cruise – sailed last week – she won't be back for three months.'

'You'll be here for three more months?' Cassie queried faintly.

'At least. You honestly didn't know? Any of it?' He pulled out to overtake a white van with an ominously smoky exhaust. 'Heck – I was sure Bennie would have shared on that.'

'Shared on what?' That grin was truly irritating. And Benita appeared to have a lot of explaining to do.

'The fact that I did a really dumb thing, of course. Tony still hasn't stopped laughing.'

Cassie felt her jaw dropping. Mr Hotshot, billionaire, everything-he-touches-turns-to-gold, could do something stupid, just like an ordinary mortal? And admit it?

She narrowed her eyes. If this was a windup— 'All right. What did you do?'

'Only let Ma back me into a corner.' He sighed. 'She

reckons I don't know how to get my hands dirty any more.'

Cassie felt a warm glow begin, in the middle of her chest. Damn, she'd always liked Mrs McQuire. And admired the way she ran her family firm, bringing up her young son single-handedly when her husband abandoned her. And carried on, after her son had done the same. Huh! McQuire men clearly had unreliability in the DNA.

'So?' she prompted brightly. 'You may as well give up the rest – or would you rather I just asked Tony?' she added innocently.

'Please!' Jake gave a faint shudder. 'Okay – okay.' He lifted his hand from the wheel, briefly, in a gesture of surrender. 'I was only dumb enough to let my *mother* bet me that I couldn't run a *real* business.'

'A *real* business.' Delight lilted through Cassie's voice. 'You mean like a detective agency?'

'Got it in one. I have three months to prove that I can run the agency and double its profits – and before you ask, I was the one who threw that in, just as a side bet, you understand. To make it more interesting.'

He'd turned towards her again. She had a flashing thought that he wasn't telling her the whole story, but it didn't matter. What he had told her was rippling laughter up through her chest in waves.

Jake waited with ostentatious patience for the hilarity to die down, attention carefully focused on the road. Cassie wiped her eyes with the back of her hand.

'That's what you get for trying to be a macho man,' she said primly.

'That's what you get for tangling with a woman with a

mind like a rattlesnake,' he countered. 'She had me hog-tied before I even saw it coming.'

'*Now* I know why you wanted to get your hands on half my fee from Benson.'

'Business, Cass, business.'

Cassie tilted her head. The vestiges of laughter were still warm under her ribs, but something uneasy was lurking too. She didn't want to voice the thought, but now that it was there ... 'Staying on for three months is all very well, but what happens then?' she asked softly. 'Running the agency is hard work. What happens if your mother decides that she wants to retire?'

Jake shrugged. 'I think that may be part of her plan, going on the cruise, to see how she likes having a life of leisure. She didn't say anything, but I've wondered if she'll want to go on.'

'If she doesn't, you'll be looking for a buyer?' Cassie's heart gave a strange little kick.

Jake's attention was on the rear view mirror. There was a police car hovering behind them. Automatically, Cassie checked their speed. They were just within the legal limit. Even so, they both let out a breath of relief when the car swooped away, after other prey.

'Irrational guilt.' Jake laughed. 'And the answer to your question is no. I don't think even my powers of persuasion could get that one past Ma. I doubt if she'll want to give up the agency entirely, even if she's less involved in the day to day stuff.' He navigated smoothly past a lorry. 'It's not a problem. I decided a while ago that I needed a change of direction in life. It might be time to come home. If she needs me, I can be here.' His mouth twisted. 'Better late than never.' He flicked Cassie a quick glance. 'It could be that I'm back in Bath for good.'

All vestiges of laughter dropped abruptly out of Cassie's chest, replaced by a flare of hope and alarm.

The trouble was she didn't know which was which.

Chapter Six

'This is the place.' Cassie leaned against the car and looked from the paper in her hand to the office block in front of her. St Paul's Cathedral loomed behind them. 'We go to the third floor, collect an envelope from a Miss Wilder and then deliver it to Chelsea.' She grimaced. 'It sounds even weirder, now we're here to do it.'

'Think of the money, Cass.'

'Mmm.' She jumped slightly as he reached over to her. 'What's this about, McQuire? You suddenly got an attack of nerves, so you need to hold my hand?'

'We're supposed to be a loving couple. Loving couples touch each other. Got to make it look genuine, Slick. Least we can do to earn our fat fee.'

Cassie gave him her narrowest stare, but resisted the urge to jerk her hand away. Instead she smiled up at him. *He has a point. And you can do the sweetheart thing – even if it does make your face ache.*

'Anything you say, Mr Benson – darling.'

'After you then, Mrs Benson – darling.'

The envelope, handed over by a harassed looking woman on the third floor, was large but light. Cassie weighed it experimentally in her hand as they walked back to the car.

'There can't be more than one sheet of paper in it. Two at the most.'

'Want to open it and find out?' Jake was scanning the street for marauding traffic wardens.

'Of course I do. But I'm not going to. And you're not either,' she warned as he reached to scoop it out of her hand. 'Give it back!'

Jake held the envelope just out of her grasp for a tantalising moment, then let her take it, pulling her towards him and giving her a quick, hard hug. She stiffened against the length of his body.

'McQuire!'

'Relax, sweetheart. Miss Wilder must have followed us down. She's in the foyer, watching us. No, don't turn around to look. Just smile lovingly up at me. That's great,' he approved as she bared her teeth at him. 'Now get in the car and let's get out of here.'

'Mr Benson? Apartment 527?' The woman at the reception desk, which guarded the foyer of the mansion block and shielded the way to the lifts, gave them a bright, professional smile. 'If you wait just a moment, I'll ring up to the apartment on the house phone, to see if anyone's there.'

'Which there shouldn't be, if he's really off climbing mountains, looking for Mrs B,' Cassie whispered to Jake, out of the corner of her mouth.

Getting no response she turned, to find him entwined in the trailing lead of a small woolly dog with a jewelled collar. The efforts of a sultry brunette to disentangle the over-extended lead seemed to be making the whole thing worse. Poorly balanced on skyscraper heels, she swayed towards Jake as the dog skittered at their feet, yapping. Irritated, Cassie leaned over and took the lead, walked around Jake, reeling it in as she went, and handed it back.

Jake, male to the core, simply stood between the two of them, grinning. With an acid look the brunette scooped up the dog and teetered off.

Jake turned towards Cassie, still grinning. For a moment the blue eyes rested on her face. Hairs stood up on the back of Cassie's neck.

'Do you think Benson will be up there?' she asked, to cover her discomfiture.

'No idea. And thanks, by the way. I was afraid we were going to have to take the dog home with us.'

Not to mention its owner. Cassie turned a snort into a cough.

The receptionist put down the phone. 'No reply, I'm afraid.' She held out her hand. 'If you'd like to leave the package, I'll make certain Mr Benson gets it.'

Cassie pulled herself together. *It was only a smile.* She looked at the receptionist and then at the envelope, reluctant to let it go.

'Oh ... yes. I suppose ...' Disappointment welled up inside her. Once the envelope was delivered, the job was over.

'You couldn't ... I mean, is it possible that Mr Benson might have left a message for us? For whoever delivered the letter?'

The receptionist frowned, clearly puzzled. 'I don't recall anything. But I will check in the office.'

She was back in less than a minute. 'No, there are no messages.' She held out her hand for the envelope. 'I assure you Mr Benson will receive it as soon as he returns.'

With a sigh Cassie handed it over. Her steps trailed as she followed Jake back to the car, parked at the side of the building.

'What's up, Slick? Mission accomplished. Money in the bank.'

'I know, it's just—'

'You didn't think it would be over this quickly,' he diagnosed. 'What were you expecting? To be handed a clue, in exchange for the envelope, like in a treasure hunt?'

'No! Oh well, all right, yes,' she admitted, seeing the scepticism in his eyes. 'Not a treasure hunt, but I was expecting *something*. And don't tell me you weren't either.'

'I'm flattered that you want to continue our partnership, of course, but it looks like it's finished now. Unless—' He cast a swift glance up at the building. 'Apartment 527. That would be the fifth floor.'

'Yes.' Cassie took a deep breath. 'Are you thinking what I'm thinking?'

'It wouldn't hurt to take a look.'

Chapter Seven

'This lift smells disgusting.'

'That's because it's normally used to transport the dustbins.' Jake inspected a cabbage leaf and a couple of used teabags that were nestling near his feet. 'Don't moan, Cass. We were lucky to find our way in so easily.'

'I'm not moaning, I'm just observing,' Cassie informed him, with as much hauteur as she could muster in such a cramped and malodorous space.

The lift, besides being small, was progressing upwards in a series of uneven lurches, which threatened to throw her unexpectedly against Jake's chest. His hand on her arm was quite comforting, in the circumstances. She was glad to note that it was causing only a mild tingling down her nerve endings.

'I suppose you're used to doing this sort of thing?' she asked, to take her mind off the tingle. 'I always thought it was terribly glamorous and exciting, the way you worked for your mum at Kings, in the school holidays,' she admitted.

Jake shook his head. 'Mostly it was making coffee and doing endless photocopying. Oh – and the sandwich run. Now *that* was downright dangerous. Those detective types! If I brought back cheese and pickle instead of tuna and cucumber my life wasn't worth a plugged nickel.'

'Idiot!' Despite herself she was grinning up at him. *Which is really not a good thing, in a confined space. Distraction, fast!* 'Er … What is a plugged nickel, anyway?'

'I don't have a clue, but I think we've arrived.'

The lift creaked to a stop and the doors wheezed open. Jake and Cassie stepped cautiously into a small, dark vestibule. A short passageway, ending in an arch and a swing door, led to a seductively lit corridor with pastel walls and thick grey carpet. Displays of silk flowers spilled out of holders set at intervals along the walls. There was no-one in sight.

They padded softly along the corridor, counting down the doors.

'523, 525, 527. This is it.' Cassie stood back. It was an ordinary panelled door, painted grey, like all the others in the corridor. 'Now what?' She put her ear experimentally to one of the panels, waving Jake to silence when he began to speak.

'Shhh!' She listened some more. After a moment she straightened up. 'I can't hear anything.'

'You could try ringing the bell.'

She gave Jake what she hoped was a withering glance, to disguise the fact that she hadn't even thought of it.

The bell pealed, long and audible.

Nothing stirred in the corridor or behind the door.

'Mr Benson?' Cassie rapped on the wood. 'Anyone at home?'

'Doesn't look like it.'

'No.' Disappointment flooded through her again. 'Well, we tried. Back to the lift, I suppose.'

'Not necessarily.' Jake was looking at the lock on the door. 'This is where it gets a little tricky. You in, Slick? Or shall we leave it?'

'What did you have in mind? Oh!' Her eyes widened as

he fished in his pocket and produced a ring of keys. 'You're not going to pick the lock!'

'What do you think?' He looked enquiringly at her.

Cassie hesitated. She'd hoped that making the delivery would somehow give her a lead. The possibility of looking around Benson's flat hadn't entered her thoughts. But now Jake was offering her the chance to investigate what was on the other side of that door ...

Surely there would be something to tell them whether Benson was genuine or not?

She knew she should say no. But to leave now ... Was she going to wake up every night, for months to come, wondering exactly what she'd been involved in? She caught her breath. 'Do it! Quick, before I have the chance to change my mind!'

'Watch to see if anyone's coming.'

Cassie glanced up and down the corridor. Her heart was thumping. She had *never* done anything like this before. *Life has certainly changed in the last twenty-four hours.*

'Ahh!' She spun round as Jake exhaled in satisfaction. 'We're in.' He pulled her to him in a rapid hug and let her go just as quickly. 'Will you write to me when we're both in jail?'

'Every day,' she agreed breathlessly. Her heart was in overdrive with excitement and apprehension. Being hugged had nothing to do with it. She left her hand where it was, in the small of Jake's back, as they stepped into the hallway of the apartment. Just for reassurance. *Or something.*

He snapped on the lights, eased the door shut and flicked the safety chain across. Cassie raised her eyebrows.

'We'll get a warning, if anyone tries to come in,' he explained.

'And we do what, exactly? Abseil down the building?'

'I was thinking more of using a sheet as a parachute. Come on, this needs to be fast,' he urged. 'I don't think my heart will last too long.'

An inappropriate impulse to put her hand on Jake's chest, to check just how fast his heart was beating, flashed into Cassie's mind. She stifled it. Her hormones were clearly over stimulated by all the excitement.

In any case, he'd stepped out of reach.

The hall was a small windowless space, with a few pleasant but unremarkable pieces of furniture. A telephone and an answering machine stood on a small table. Cassie inspected them. The message light on the answer machine showed zero. No messages.

Jake had his head in a large cupboard. She moved to stand by his shoulder.

'Nothing much. Coats and an ironing board,' he reported. He held up a button, pointing at an old raincoat. 'This was in the pocket. I don't think it's a clue.'

Cassie rolled her eyes and pushed open the nearest door.

The rest of the flat was furnished in the same bland style as the hall.

'It looks more like a place that's rented out fully furnished than someone's home,' Cassie remarked.

Jake nodded. He was rifling efficiently through a small desk in the sitting room.

'Shouldn't you have gloves? You know, for fingerprints?' she asked, when he looked blankly at her.

'Who's going to look for them? We're not planning to

steal anything are we? Unless you have your heart set on that revolting brass owl on the windowsill?'

'I think it's rather cute.'

It was Jake's turn to roll his eyes. He finished rapidly with the desk. 'Nothing personal. No bills, or bank statements or anything like that. Just this.' He pointed to the receipt for the purchase of euros and a coloured card with the name and address of a restaurant on it.

'San Remo?' Cassie read aloud. 'Is that in Italy?'

'Yes.' Jake inclined his head. 'It might have something to do with that.'

There was a book draped, face down, over the arm of a chair.

'Guidebook to the Italian Riviera, open at—'Cassie tipped the book over. '—the entry for San Remo. Um ... Mr Benson is supposed to be looking for Mrs Benson in Scotland.'

'Scotland is a long way from Italy.'

'Holiday planning?'

'Maybe.'

Leaving Jake in the main room, Cassie drifted into the bathroom. She inspected the single toothbrush and the towel on the rail. An examination of the cabinet over the sink revealed only a few men's toiletries.

'I'm beginning to get a strange feeling about Mrs Benson,' she called out to Jake. By the sound of it, he was opening and shutting the cupboards in the kitchen. She didn't know whether he'd heard her.

Cassie went back to the hall. She hesitated, with her hand on the door to what must be the bedroom. The hushed atmosphere in the flat was getting to her. It was all so quiet. There was no noise from the corridor, and only a faint buzz of traffic from the busy street below. A shiver breathed on the back of her neck. The whole place was eerie.

Cautiously she pushed open the door in front of her.

It was just a bedroom. Rather a nice one, with light streaming in through long, triple-glazed windows. The bed was freshly made. The duvet, and the white cotton sheet which was folded over the top of it, were smooth and unused. The wardrobe and the drawers were empty.

'Any luck?' Jake appeared in the doorway, making her jump. A hot, prickling sensation ran over her skin. It was her nerves. *Nothing to do with having Jake on one side of you and a bed on the other.*

'Nope.' She moved away from the bed. It brought her closer to Jake, but that couldn't be helped. 'I'm beginning to wonder if anyone lives here.' She gestured to the empty dressing table. 'There isn't even a trace of dust. It's probably cleaned and the linen changed every day by a maid service. The bed hasn't been slept in and all the stuff in the bathroom is bone dry. Doesn't look as if it's been used for days. And there's no sign of a woman anywhere.'

'Observant.' The approval in Jake's face gave Cassie a little lick of pleasure in the pit of her stomach. 'So – looks like Benson is not what he appears and Mrs Benson may not exist.'

'And someone, possibly Benson, has more than a passing interest in the Riviera.'

'Can't say I blame him. It's very nice down there at this time of the year.'

Jake was walking round the bed, examining the carpet.

'I wouldn't know.' Cassie watched him, frowning. 'Are you looking for anything in particular?'

'No. I was just wondering—'

The doorbell rang.

Cassie froze. Jake swung round to face the door of the room. The bell pealed, longer and louder, and the front door rattled.

'Mr Benson?' A man's voice. The door rattled again.

Then there was the unmistakable sound of a key being inserted in the lock.

Cassie's eyes flicked up to meet Jake's, in a second of blind panic. Then she was moving, throwing down her bag and reaching up to the ribbon that was holding back her hair.

'Move it, McQuire!' She shook her hair free. 'Don't just stand there. Take your clothes off.'

Chapter Eight

It took two beats for Jake to follow Cassie's thoughts. Then he was yanking at the knot of his tie and shrugging himself out of his jacket. He thrust both into Cassie's outstretched hands.

'Shoes.' She kicked her own into an artistic heap in the hall. 'And unbutton your shirt!'

'Mr Benson? Is everything all right in there?'

The door was straining on its chain as Jake hopped from one foot to the other, flinging his shoes and socks unceremoniously into a corner. 'Got to go, Slick!'

'Hold on.' Cassie ran her finger over her mouth, smudging gloss off her lips and on to Jake's. They were warm and firm and she tried not to notice. 'Okay, go.' She backed off as he leaned towards her. His eyes had lights in them that she didn't want to think about. 'Go on,' she hissed. 'Remember – think sex,' she threw the instruction over her shoulder as she turned to haul the covers off the bed.

'All the time, darling.' Jake's laughter drifted back to her as he headed for the front door.

Cassie kicked the bedroom door shut behind him, sliding out of her dress and her bra slip at the same time, her ears straining as she dumped them on top of Jake's jacket on a convenient chair. She made out the sound of the chain being removed, followed by muffled voices, as she mussed and dented pillows.

It was about time for her entrance.

A quick look in the mirror had her rumpling her hair some more, before dragging the sheet off the bed and draping it around herself, anchoring it securely under her arms. She paused at the door, to take a quick, nerve-steadying breath. Then she threw it open and sashayed into the hall.

'What's the matter darling?' She gave what she hoped was a breathy giggle. 'Are we getting into trouble?'

'No, sweetheart.' A uniformed security guard filled the doorway. Jake was standing just inside it, one hand braced casually against the door. Cassie's breath hitched a little in her throat. The relaxed stance, the appreciative gleam in his eyes as he smiled at her, the unbuttoned shirt. Something hot coiled in the pit of her stomach. 'Just a routine security check. The officer noticed the light under the door. Good old Gerry didn't mention that we might be using his place,' Jake explained.

For a second Cassie stared at him blankly. Panic hovered. Then her memory kicked in. Gerald Benson, resident of the apartment.

'That man is *soooo* forgetful.' Another throaty giggle. *Oh God, is that hysteria?* The security man's pop-eyed stare had flipped from her to the rumpled bed. She'd been especially careful to leave the door to the bedroom wide open behind her. *Result!*

Tripping over to Jake she leaned in, gave the guard her very best smile, and let the sheet slip a fraction.

'I'm sure you told the nice man we're not really doing anything naughty.' She upped the wattage on the smile and appreciated the stunned expression on the guard's face. She was getting into this. 'We aren't, are we Baby-cakes?'

She pouted at the Nice Man, and felt Baby-cakes flinch in a most satisfactory way.

'Not at all, Sugar-pie.' Jake reached out a lazy hand and scooped her closer, nestling his face into her hair.

Jake's body warmth, and the familiar way she fitted into the crook of his arm, sent a disturbing quiver up Cassie's spine. She sucked in air. *This is not for real. This is just acting.*

'I'm sure he understands perfectly.' Cassie felt as well as heard the tremor of laughter in Jake's voice. His chest vibrated, close to her ear.

'Um ... well. Yes, uh, sir. As everything is in order ... well, I'll just be getting along now ...'

The guard, red in the face, began to back away, but not before Jake reached out and tucked a folded banknote into his breast pocket. 'A little something for your trouble – Carl.' Jake read the name badge on the man's shirt. 'I'm sure we can count on your discretion. And of course I'll let Gerry know what an excellent job you're doing, taking care of the place.'

'Oh! Yes. Thank you, sir. Not at all, sir.' Carl backed into the corridor. 'I hope you have ... I mean ... er. Goodbye now, sir, miss.'

Gently but firmly, Jake closed the door on him.

There was a second of total silence.

Then Cassie's breath came out in a whoop, half relief, half laughter. She sagged away from Jake's embrace.

'Sugar-pie!'

'Baby-cakes!' Jake retaliated, grinning.

'Oh.' Her voice wavered. 'The look on that poor man's face.' She sobered up abruptly. 'I hope he doesn't tell anyone.'

Jake snorted. 'Of course he will! The money will hold him for a while, but it's too good a tale to keep to himself. Come on—' He stared at her. 'Catching a couple in a borrowed flat, having a lunchtime quickie?'

'You think—Oh ...' Cassie covered her face with her hands.

'Don't worry about it. I doubt if Gerald Benson will get to hear of it.' Jake took hold of her shoulder, drawing her towards him and gently lifting her fingers away from her cheek. His eyes burned a dark, intense blue. '*You* were brilliant. You haven't lost it, Slick. None of it.'

'Jake?' Confused, Cassie dropped her hands, tried to take a pace away, but his hold on her tightened before she could move. He was pulling her into him with one hand, tipping up her chin with the other. For one brief, dizzy second, memory almost overwhelmed her. She *so* wanted this. Then realisation kicked in.

'Jake! No!' She pushed against him, but it was already too late. He was close.

Too close.

He lowered his head.

His mouth had been places and learned things since the last time he'd kissed her.

Wicked things.

Like how to close over hers so completely, so perfectly, there was no breath free to argue. Like how to nudge and nuzzle his way inside, with heat and charm, so that all coherent thought evaporated, straight out of her ears. Little spurts and sparks flew over her skin, fizzing where they landed.

Wildfire.

Her nerve endings were going to fry. *She couldn't wait.*

With a small moan that caught in the back of her throat, she melted towards Jake's body. Her fingers found their own way under his open shirt to his chest. They knew this skin, wanted it. She reached his shoulders, held on, let herself sink.

In the tiny part of Jake's brain that was still capable of coherent thought, a flare of panic sizzled. *This isn't the plan!* His three functioning brain cells were screaming at him. *Way too much, way too soon!* He'd lit a match and got a volcano back at him. His senses were turning to smoke. Where had all this heat come from? And then – *Do you care?*

Her body, when it drifted into his, damn near buckled his knees. He was deep in her mouth and wanting deeper, more. He pulled her against him, bracing his feet to lift her, carry her back to the bedroom—

The phone rang.

Cassie found herself plastered against the wall. She didn't know whether she'd jumped or Jake had pushed. He looked as dazed she felt. His eyes were almost black, and clouded.

She found enough breath to speak. 'We can't answer it.'

'No,' he agreed, hoarsely.

Cassie saw the focus coming back into his eyes. A stab of regret arced through her. She pulled herself up sharply, swaying a little. *You don't mean that.*

'The machine will pick it up.' Jake straightened, pushing his hair off his face.

On the sixth ring the answer phone cut in, with a whirr and a hiss. The outgoing message – was it Benson? – and the caller's response were made indistinct by crackling noises. Cassie recognised a few words. The caller was speaking in Italian.

'Jake?'

He held up his hand for silence, concentrating. Cassie waited, biting her lip. The machine clicked off.

'Did you get that?' she asked.

'Not all of it. Too fast. It was something about a meeting. Hold on.'

He scooted into the bedroom and was back in a second, holding a tiny voice recorder. Cassie started to smile as he pressed play, positioning the recorder to capture the message.

'Clever,' she approved, as the answer-phone clicked off again.

Jake turned to grin at her and she suddenly remembered that most of what she was wearing was a bed sheet. 'Um.'

Simultaneously, they both heaved in a breath.

The residue of heat shimmered in the air for a second.

Jake shook his head, as if to clear it. 'I'll have someone translate it in full. Right now I think we'd better get out of here, Slick.'

'So do I. And if you don't stop calling me Slick, I shall have to kill you!'

Cassie slithered into her underwear and her dress almost as fast as she'd slithered out of them. She flinched slightly as she felt Jake's hands on her back, but he was only zipping her up.

'Er, thanks.' When she turned, she found he'd dressed just as rapidly as she had. She didn't know whether she was relieved or sorry. *Excuse me? Of course you're relieved.*

'We'd better make the bed.'

'Um, yes.' She knew she was going pink. *Making* the bed hadn't been in her mind a few moments ago. Her nerve endings were still tingling. Keeping her distance, she scooped up the duvet and pillows. Working together they quickly had the thing reassembled.

'Is everything back in place?'

'In the room, yes.'

Cassie's eyes darted up to meet Jake's.

'I think we just shifted the parameters of this business arrangement, Cass.' He reached out and pulled her gently towards him. She surprised herself by letting him.

'Then we're going to have to shift them back again.' She wasn't that far gone that she couldn't defend herself, even if being in his arms did feel too damn good for a steady heartbeat.

'Can we?'

'Yes.' She detached herself from his hold, not without a pang. 'You keep your hands to yourself, McQuire, and I'll do the same.'

'Anything you say, Sugar-pie.' He held up his hands, to show her, fingers spread.

Despite herself, Cassie felt a bubble of laughter welling up.

'Come on, let's get out of here, before anything else happens!'

Chapter Nine

They were rounding the building and heading to the car when they ran into the woman from the reception desk.

'Oh! Hello again.' She looked surprised to see them. Cassie muttered something about grabbing lunch, and the woman's puzzlement evaporated into a smile. 'I'm glad I met you.' She was positively beaming now. 'You don't have to worry about your envelope. Mr Benson dropped in, about ten minutes after you left, and collected it.'

'Dropped in?' Cassie's chin came up. 'Is he still around?'

'Oh no. He had a friend waiting in the car. He just picked up the package and they drove off together.' The woman frowned. 'Why do you—'

'That's good to know.' Jake intervened, throwing the woman a smile that made her blink. He grasped Cassie by the arm, swinging her in the direction of the car. 'We appreciate you telling us, don't we, darling?' He bent close to Cassie's ear. 'Leave it, or she's going to smell a rat.'

Cassie's jaw stiffened mutinously. She sensed that Jake was holding his breath, body tense. Much as she liked provoking that feeling, she knew he was right. Reluctantly she relaxed, and felt him do the same.

'Of course we appreciate it, *darling*.' She twisted out of his grip and stalked off. Jake gave the woman one last smile and followed.

Neither spoke until they were back in the Bentley.

'I don't believe it! We were wasting our time upstairs,

and he was *here*! We missed him by *ten* minutes!' Cassie groaned.

'Luck of the draw, Sli—' Jake swallowed the rest as she turned twin laser scalpels on him, but his own eyes glittered. 'I wouldn't say we wasted our time in the apartment,' he suggested provocatively.

He got a huff of annoyance and a hunched shoulder in response.

'Do your seat belt up.' He guided the car into the traffic. 'Please?'

Cassie slid the belt around her. It was childish and unprofessional to sulk, even if frustration did make her want to hit something. *To be that close!*

'I'm curious. What would you have done if we had spotted him?'

'I— we could have—' She stopped. 'All right—' She cast Jake an exasperated look. '—I have no idea. Don't laugh!'

'Wouldn't dream of it.'

Cassie studied his profile with suspicion. That might be a twitch of the lip. She decided to ignore it. She looked out of the window instead, studying the road signs.

'This isn't the way back to the motorway. Where are we going?'

'You said something about lunch just now. Sounds good to me.'

'Oh, well … I think we should be getting back. I have work.' Now the excitement was over she ought to get this thing finished. She really didn't want to have lunch with Jake in some expensive restaurant, with everyone assuming they were a couple.

'We both have to eat,' he pointed out reasonably. 'At one time you were always hungry.'

'That was then.' And it wasn't just food that she'd been hungry for. She shoved that thought away, glaring at a passing pedestrian, who was using a crossing in front of them. The woman gave a start, and began to trot towards the opposite pavement.

'Don't try to kill innocent people with the death stare, Cass, it looks bad.'

He'd always been far too attuned to her mind and her body language. She transferred the stare to him, narrowing her eyes. He laughed.

'We'll eat. Then, if you want to practise killing with a single glance, I'm all yours.'

The thought that he might be sent a shiver across her abdomen.

Jake's choice for lunch was a complete surprise. She'd expected something over the top, where waiters spoke in hushed, reverent tones and her version of the menu came without prices on it. Instead she found herself in a cheerfully crowded restaurant on the South Bank, sitting on a bench at a long table.

They ate moules and frites, the house special for the day. Jake tried to steal her fries, until she threatened to stick her fork into him.

'Stop it!' She grazed the prongs lightly over his knuckles. He moved his hand, but brought the other up quickly to capture a handful from her bowl, before she could react.

'Slowing down, Cass?' he asked, around a mouthful of *her* lunch.

'You just got sneakier.' She moved the bowl out of his reach.

'Guilty as charged.' Laughing, Jake waved to a passing waiter and ordered an extra portion of fries and a side order of garlic bread. It arrived promptly and they munched in companionable silence. When he'd cleared his plate and a good portion of the bread, Jake sat back and watched Cassie finishing her last delicious mouthfuls. 'I've been meaning to ask – the concierge thing? How did that happen? It's a good idea.'

'And I can't have good ideas?'

'Did I say that?' He shook his head. 'Always so prickly, Cass. I'm not an enemy.'

'This, from the man who tried to steal my lunch.' She detached a mussel from its shell, and popped it into her mouth.

'Go on, tell me about the business. I'm interested.'

Cassie shrugged. 'There are a lot of people who need chores doing – jobs and errands they don't have the talent or the time for. I like organising things. I started arranging events and social stuff while I was at university.' *Keeping busy takes your mind off a broken heart.* 'It just grew slowly from that.'

'Your parents helped with funds?'

She shook her head and reached for a piece of bread to soak up the juice from her plate. 'They needed all their resources to buy a place in Spain. They've retired there. I worked a whole raft of temp jobs to get the start up money – office work, barista, bar maid, waitressing, dog walking, pet sitting – all of it was good experience. Then I did a couple of business courses. We were finally able to launch the year before last. It was a good time – the run up to Christmas – lots of people with far too many things on their "To Do" lists. The overheads aren't huge, but we had to have an office, a couple of second hand computers, stationery and advertising. It mounts up.' She gave a shrug that was a fraction too close to a shudder for her peace of mind. 'We've been running as close to the bone as possible, to get some resources behind us and plough money back. And it was working.' She sighed. 'I was looking forward to getting a couple of those whizzy gadgets – a smart phone, a tablet computer. But now …'

'Now you have Benson's money.'

'Mmm.' She speared her last mussel.

'It would buy plenty of er … *whizzy* gadgets.'

Cassie was spared an explanation of her deal with Benita over the money by the waiter, pausing by the table to check whether they wanted more drinks. Cassie declined a repeat of her mineral water. She saw Jake hesitate. She'd tried a sip of the locally brewed beer he'd ordered. She'd approved his choice, but drinking alcohol in the middle of the day made her sleepy. She had work to get back to. There wouldn't be much of the afternoon left, but she'd have to make the most of what there was.

'Have another,' she suggested, looking up from under her lashes, deliberately provocative. 'I'll drive home.'

'Okay.' Jake slid the car keys across the table, and ordered another beer.

Cassie knew her eyes were popping. She couldn't help it.

'You'll let me drive your car? The Bentley?'

'Why not?'

'I might drive it into a tree.'

'Do you drive into many trees?'

'No!'

'Then I reckon we're pretty safe.' He was watching her with that half amused look that made her want to thump him and kiss him all at the same time. She closed her hand over the car keys instead.

'I thought all guys considered their cars as phallic symbols – you know, extensions of their—' She flinched, biting her lip as the second beer landed in front of Jake. The waiter was grinning and she could feel her neck going pink. *Now look what he made me do!*

'You've been mixing with the wrong sort of man, Cass.' Jake took a slug of the beer. 'It doesn't threaten me to have a woman drive me. I don't have any problem with my masculinity.'

Cassie let out a sigh. *Isn't that the truth?*

Expecting a wrangle over the bill, Cassie slapped her money down on the table as soon as the waiter delivered it. Jake added his share and gave her a smile like a wolf. 'Shall we go?'

The Bentley handled like a dream.

Jake watched as she navigated them deftly through a maze of one-way streets. 'The hell with driving into trees. You chauffeur clients around, don't you?'

Rumbled, Cassie nodded. 'Did an advanced driving course last year.'

'But presumably you don't use that old heap of yours for clients?'

'Archie,' she corrected automatically. 'He's a good little work horse.' She grinned when Jake snorted. 'We use a hire car, or occasionally the client's own, if it's a port or airport

66

drop or pick up. The week before last the client had a Lamborghini. With the scissor doors,' she added smugly.

'Been there, done that.' Jake smoothly capped her taunt. 'This was more suitable for ferrying Ma to the hospital.'

Cassie nodded. 'Good choice. It's a lovely car.'

Jake inclined his head, accepting the compliment. After a few moments, satisfied that Cassie was comfortable with the controls, he settled down and went to sleep, leaving her to commune with the car. She communed, just under the speed limit, for a long stretch of motorway. It felt *really* good. She'd have a bit of explaining to do when she next slipped behind Archie's wheel.

Jake opened his eyes as Cassie brought the car to rest in a parking space, right outside the office, that had miraculously opened up just as they entered the street.

'Right ... Um ... Thanks for your help.' Cassie squirmed, uncharacteristically uncertain. Should she just get out? Offer to shake hands? What?

Jake solved the problem.

He leaned over, pulled her into his arms and kissed her, very hard and very thoroughly. Cassie's hands fluttered ineffectually at his back, then buried themselves, of their own accord, in his hair.

When Jake eventually let her come up for air there was only one coherent thought in her head.

Do it again.

Now.

Her bones melted into the leather seat as Jake read her mind. She was dazed, her head ringing, when he finally let go. Even through the haze, triumph welled in her chest when she saw that his eyes were dark and clouded. *Not so cool now, McQuire.*

Her own senses were swamped. The fierce craving to press herself close to him, to surrender, to let him do whatever he wanted, just so long as he didn't stop— *Oh no!*

Face flaming, she was out of the car and on the pavement as fast as her wobbly legs would carry her. Her heart hammered as the passenger door opened. Jake was coming after her. He was going to kiss her, right here in the street, in front of passers-by and potential clients and – everyone.

The sense of anti-climax when he crossed to the driver's side, and opened the door, had her stomach swooping almost down to her unsteady knees.

Belatedly, temper flared. 'Don't you *ever* do that again!'

Jake was shaking his head. 'I don't make promises if I don't intend to keep them, Slick.'

'Since when? I don't *want* you to kiss me.'

He gave her a long, slow look. Then he smiled, in a way that very nearly dislocated her toes.

'Fine. Whatever you say.' He folded himself behind the wheel. 'Bennie has my number, if you need me. You remember what I said before? Any reason. Day or night. Bye Cass.' He was closing the door. 'You know, you're very sexy when you're mad. What the Americans call hot. Very hot.'

The car was pulling away before Cassie could think of a retort, and even then it was only a string of curses.

Recollecting herself, she looked around and then up at the office building. No one seemed to have noticed her embarrassment. She pushed open the red door and all but threw herself up the stairs. Jake McQuire would rot in hell before she'd speak to him again.

Jake guided the car through the late afternoon traffic, reviewing the day. A half smile turned up his mouth. Cassie had got his kit off, and her own, he had kissed her three times, they'd done a little burglary and eaten lunch. Plus he'd made her as mad as a nest of hornets.

It was an excellent start.

Chapter Ten

Fizzing with adrenaline, Cassie had disposed of two outstanding assignments and was reaching for the file on a third when Benita put her head around the door.

'I'm off. Don't stay all night.'

'Uhh? Oh!' Cassie glanced at the clock. 'That time already?'

'Absolutely.'

'See you in the morning, then.'

Bennie clattered down the stairs. Cassie opened the folder she'd pulled towards her. It was a new job. A recommendation. Cassie let out a contented sigh. They really were the best kind, when one satisfied customer passed her name to another. And she *loved* vicarious house hunting. The client would be flying in from Hong Kong at the end of the month and wanted a short-list of suitable properties prepared, with arrangements made for viewings. The list of essential requirements was long, and very specific – but at the price he was prepared to pay, it wasn't going to be a problem. Cassie made a few notes in the margins, things to check, people to ring, then leaned back in her chair. The building was quiet. The shop below was shut for the night.

She got up and went to the window, looking out, absently rubbing her thumb over the glass.

She'd cleared some work, and she had a satisfying job to look forward to—and yet …

She knew what was bothering her, hovering at the

edge of her mind, like a small black cloud. It was disappointment, mixed with a trace of apprehension. The Benson thing was over. She hadn't been able to find out anything worthwhile, despite her plan to investigate. Jake had collected all the information about the Riviera, but she didn't see how she could make any use of it. Benson had the envelope, and whatever had been in it, and the trail was cold. She wished now that she'd ignored her principles and taken a peek.

Of course, her disappointment had nothing to do with losing her reason to see Jake again. Why would she want to? All that was over, long ago. He'd been her first love – but hey, they'd been kids, buzzing with hormones, experimenting on each other's bodies. Back then she'd thought it was going to last forever. And that she was going to die when he left. Romeo and Juliet. *Kids' stuff*.

She had survived. She'd kept her pride. Even Benita didn't know quite how thoroughly Jake had trampled on her heart. The betrayal still rankled though, even now. She didn't want to tangle with him again. And she was *so* not still carrying a torch for him. Not even a spent match. Yeah – he'd matured into a mouth-watering hunk. So? He'd kissed her, and she had responded. She was female and healthy and he knew what he was doing with that mouth. *Oh boy did he know!* It had felt good. She could be honest there. But it wasn't going to happen again.

Jake was up to something. She didn't want to know what it was. He was probably just amusing himself, trying to see how far he could push her. If he was imagining that he'd sweet talk her back into bed with him, he was mistaken. He would be gone soon, and then she could relax again.

She frowned. He'd said he might be back to stay, but that couldn't be right. He had business interests all over the world, and a penthouse in New York. The stuff about staying had to be a lie, and yet the Jake she'd known had never been a liar. She remembered only two occasions, in all the time she'd known him. Once when he'd said her hair looked great, after she'd had the haircut from hell. Everyone else had told her the truth – that it was the pits.

And then there was the other time. The big one. He'd promised to be back from New York in six weeks and had sworn to write every day. She'd believed him then, and she'd been a fool. He'd gone for good, without even saying a proper good-bye.

'Face it, Travers. People change. And you have lousy taste in men.'

She crossed to the desk and rummaged in a drawer, unearthing the file she'd opened on Jason Fairbrook. This was her latest attempt at a love life, reduced to one thin folder in her desk. She flicked the file open. She needed to give some more time to this, to track Jason down and force him to return her money. *But not tonight.*

She rotated her neck, working out the stiffness from sitting at her desk. Maybe she should take Jake up on his offer. Maybe a little recreational sex with a prime male was just what she needed to work out the kinks. *Not.*

With a sigh she threw the Fairbrook folder back into the drawer and went to lock up.

* * *

72

By morning Cassie's disappointment and unease had turned to fretting. What had been in that envelope? How bad could it be? She and Jake had probably been filmed by security cameras collecting and delivering it. Both their fingerprints would be all over it.

Fingerprints.

They'd been in Benson's apartment. They'd been seen. The security guard – Carl – Jake might be confident that he wouldn't speak to Benson, but what if he did? The flat didn't look as if Benson spent much time there, but he only had to be there for a moment – the wrong moment – to talk to Carl. And then how long would it take, to link the whole thing back to her?

Why the hell did you get yourself into this?

She looked at the phone, tempted to call Jake, just for the satisfaction of yelling at him and blasting off some of her worry. Her hand slid out, then shot back. She'd eat *glass* before she'd ask Bennie for the number. She *didn't* want to talk to Jake. And, of course, she had no interest *at all* in the message in Italian on the answer phone

The Benson case is done. Old news. Jake McQuire doesn't matter at all. If he walked in here now, you'd simply freeze him back out again.

The arrival of an American visitor, trying to find her English roots, gave Cassie a welcome distraction.

'I'm with a group, on a tour. Ten days in England. I just love it here. And my great grandma came from Somerset, and I promised myself to find out more about her ... I thought there would be time ... but there's just so much to see ... And we were having breakfast across the street, and I noticed your sign, so I came on up.'

She finally paused for breath, frowning. 'A concierge service. Can you do that, honey? Look for a person's family?'

'We do our best to supply whatever a client wants – within reason.' *And sometimes without it.* 'I don't do that kind of work myself, but I can certainly find you an expert. They would do the research and send you a report.'

'There are people who do that? Now *that* would be exactly what I need.'

Cassie grinned. The day was looking up. 'Why don't you sit down and give me a few details?'

The prospective client, whose name was Thelma, was getting up to leave when Cassie heard voices in the outer office.

Oh no.

Oh yes.

After a perfunctory knock, the door swung open and Jake strolled in. As if he owned the place. Cassie gave him a glare to melt granite. Clearly McQuire's head was harder than granite.

'I have a client with me,' she pointed out, channelling ice queen mode. She would *not* let him get to her. She was going to keep her cool, if it *killed* her.

'Oh— but we were just finished, honey.' Thelma looked up at Jake, eyes widening. Jake gave her the slow version of The McQuire Smile. Thelma's eyes got even wider. Cassie gritted her teeth, rage bubbling. *Cool, calm, chill. Think of icebergs.*

Thelma looked at Jake, then swivelled to look at Cassie.

Whatever she saw, it made her laugh. Still laughing

and shaking her head, she wiggled her fingers at Cassie, sidestepped neatly around Jake, and left them to it.

Jake knew he was a coward. When Bennie told him Cass had a client with her, his heart had lifted. He'd figured there was less chance of her throwing something at him, on sight, if there was someone else present. Now he closed the door and braced himself for the onslaught.

It didn't come.

Cassie had turned away from him and was staring at the book case. Jake propped himself against the wall and stuck his hands in his belt.

New game.

Actually, he liked this. Nothing with sharp edges was coming at his head and he had the chance to study Cassie's profile. She'd always been especially pretty when she was mad at him. Now she was stunning. *Which probably means she's a lot more than mad. What comes after mad? Incandescent, maybe?*

Air compressed in his lungs. She'd grown up into one heck of a woman. Yesterday he'd kissed her. And to make it worse, they'd both enjoyed it. She'd had all night to stew on that one, and the result was unlikely to be pretty. Right now she was probably ready to tear his ears off, with her bare hands.

Time for a little diversion strategy.

He peeled himself away from the wall, took an envelope out of his pocket and tossed it down on the desk.

'Right, Slick, get your passport.'

'What?' Cassie's head jerked towards him. Jake's heart jittered. *Oh wow! How did I forget how lovely her eyes are?*

75

And now she was confused, as well as mad. *Is this good or bad?*

When she folded her arms and gave a theatrical sigh, he let out a fraction of his own pent-up breath. *Good –ish. No violence. Yet.*

'Jake, what the hell are you talking about?'

'Passport. You know. Little booklet thing, with a photo that makes you look like an axe murderer? You use it to travel from country to country.' She was staring at him now as if he'd just landed from a distant planet. 'Cass, you do have a passport, don't you?'

'Of course I do.'

Chapter Eleven

She did have a passport. Somewhere. Not that it was any of Jake's business. Cassie eyed the envelope that he'd dumped in front of her. The flap was open, but she couldn't see inside. She was damned if she would show enough interest to pick it up.

After a couple of beats, Jake did it, tipping the contents out on the desk.

'Plane tickets? Car hire?' Cassie prodded the papers with one finger. 'Rental agreement for a villa?' She couldn't keep the hint of a squeak out of her voice. 'McQuire, what the hell is all this?'

'You want to find out what Benson is up to, don't you?'

'You know I do.'

'Then this is how we do it.' He pulled back his cuff, to check his watch. 'Better get a move on, Slick, if you want to pack a bag. We're booked on the one o'clock flight to Nice.'

The gasp came all the way up from Cassie's toes. 'What! I can't just drop everything and go to Nice.' Her head whirled. 'In case you haven't noticed, I run a business here. I have work to do.'

'Bring it with you.'

'Wha—' Cassie shut her mouth with a snap. She had to stop saying what, every time Jake said something. 'How?'

'A lot of your stuff is done over the phone and on

the internet, right?' He looked levelly at her. 'They have phones in Europe, Cass. Internet connections. All you have to do is bring your laptop.'

Cassie seized the first objection, one of many, that jostled to the front of her brain. All this was moving way too fast. 'I don't have a laptop.' *Well, not one that actually works.* Jake gave an elaborate sigh. 'Then you can borrow mine.' He was stowing the travel documents in his jacket pockets.

'I have to be here, to meet clients. That woman just now—'

'Benita can handle it. Just like she does all the other times when you're not in the office,' Jake cut in. 'Quit stalling Cassie. If you want to pack, then we'd better get to it. Of course, if you want me to lend you my toothbrush as well as the computer, then we can move right along to the airport,' he offered silkily.

Cassie made a low growling noise in her throat. Jake had her cornered, and he knew it. Benson had been *her* client. If anyone was going to investigate him, she was. She wasn't about to let Jake take the thing over. And if she didn't go with McQuire, he'd do it alone.

She did her best to deal with the tiny part of her that wanted to get excited about going to the Riviera, with Jake, to solve a mystery. *You don't want to be with Jake. It's just a job. And —wait a minute – maybe the chance to trace Jason's aunt?* Cassie let out a long breath. *Now that would be a really good reason to go with Jake.*

The thought warmed her as she began throwing files into her briefcase. She wasn't going to look at Jake yet though. She just *knew* he'd be grinning.

'This is about that recording, right?' She stopped stuffing files to heft snooty eyebrows at him. He *was* grinning. *Damn.* 'What was on it?'

'I'll tell you in the car.' He reached out to take the case from her.

Cassie stiffened. 'I can carry my own bag, McQuire.'

'I know,' he agreed. 'But why bother when you have some poor sap to carry it for you?'

To struggle would be undignified. Cassie trailed after Jake, eyes drawn to the breadth of his shoulders, in what was undoubtedly a criminally expensive suit. She'd never use the words "Jake McQuire" and "poor sap" in the same sentence. Jake was simply too much man.

And isn't that a big part of the problem?

She'd assumed that Jake would wait in the car while she threw things into a suitcase. Instead he followed her into her tiny flat and ... loomed ... while she packed. There was no other word for it. He was so damn – big.

'Passport.' She held it up in triumph, after a quick hunt in the sideboard and a surreptitious check, to see that it hadn't expired. Jake nodded, then went back to his inspection of her books and pictures.

Cassie raided the bathroom, before darting into the bedroom. A quick glance showed her that Jake had found her collection of vampire novels. *He ought to be right at home there.*

She dragged a suitcase from under the bed, swept an armful of clothes off hangers and out of drawers, and dumped them into the open bag. Tossing in some underwear, she was done. She lugged the bag into the sitting room, sighing noisily as Jake picked it up with no more effort than if it had been empty.

Back in the car she pounced. 'So – what was on the recording? Why are we flying to France? The message was in Italian.' She noticed the suspicion of a grin. 'What's funny?'

'You haven't changed. Straight to what you want.'

Once, what you wanted was him.

'Huh! I can do subtle if I have to.' If he hadn't been driving she'd have kicked his shin. *Immature, but satisfying.* She seemed to be regressing to age seventeen. She shivered. *At age seventeen, Jake was your whole world.* 'Stop messing about, McQuire. Tell me!'

'Translation.' He took his hand off the wheel, to pass over a sheet of paper. Their fingers touched. Something warm shimmied up Cassie's arm. She unfolded the sheet, chewing her bottom lip. There was a brief geographical note at the top of the page. The recording referred to the Italian city of San Remo. San Remo was close to the border with France, which made Nice the nearest airport. As for the rest …

'Villa Verdi?'

'Outskirts of San Remo, the Italian side of the border.'

'And this restaurant – Poisson d'Avril?'

'Menton, the French side.'

'And the bit about the casino?'

Jake shrugged. 'I haven't a clue, but there's a casino in San Remo, and Monte Carlo isn't that far away. Take your pick.'

'So – Benson may be staying at this Villa Verdi. Do you really think he's there?'

'Well – someone connected to him might be.'

Cassie sniffed. 'It could be anyone – his boss, or his dentist, or his dear old granny!'

'Well if it is, we can ask them where he is, can't we?' Jake suggested.

Cassie threw him an exasperated look. 'Oh yeah. Why didn't I think of that? Just pitch up at the door, do we? Sorry to bother you, sir/madam, but do you happen to know a man called Benson, and if you do, could you tell us where he is? Only he paid my associate and me a lot of money to do a very simple job and now we're wondering what we've got ourselves into.'

'When you put it like that …' Jake cocked an eyebrow at her and laughed. 'I'm sure we'll think of something when the time comes.'

'It would be better to have a plan,' Cassie grumbled, but settled back in her seat. They'd crack it. *Together*. The word had a funny resonance, sending a strange sensation up her spine. She wriggled to get comfortable again.

'This place you've rented? It's close to the Villa Verdi?'

'So I understand.'

'And do we have a reservation at the Poisson d'Avril next Monday?'

'Nope – too obvious. We have a reservation at the place across the street.'

Cassie digested this. 'You have a very efficient organisation.'

Jake flashed her an amused glance. 'Compliments, Slick?'

'Credit where it's due.' She shifted uneasily. 'All this must be costing a packet. I want a proper account. I pay my own way.'

'It's coming out of my share of the fee.'

'I can't let you—'

'Indulge me, Cass.' The unexpected note of steel in Jake's voice made her look over at him. His eyes were on the road. His profile was hard, all planes and angles.

Cassie opened her mouth, sucked in air, and closed it again. Then she spoke, 'If this whole thing is a wild goose chase, you will have wasted your money.'

'I might,' he agreed. 'But at least we'll have had a few days in the sun.'

Chapter Twelve

'This way.' Jake hooked his fingers under Cassie's arm and steered her past the line of people she'd been about to join.

'This is the queue for the flight to Nice,' she objected.

'I think you'll find we need to check in here.' Jake pulled the ticket print-outs from his jacket pocket and smiled at the woman behind the desk. Cassie stared at the sign above her head with mounting horror.

'First class! You got us first class seats!'

'You have a problem with that? What am I saying? Of course you have! You have a problem with everything I do.' Jake exhaled heavily. 'You don't have to come with me, Cass.'

He turned and met her eyes, full on. Cassie felt dizzy. She tried to swallow. How had her tongue got stuck to the roof of her mouth? When Jake looked at her like that ...

'I do,' she managed, breathless. 'I want to come with you.'

Cassie shut her eyes. *Is there really any point in arguing? You're getting on that plane. Better to save your energy for when it really matters.*

Opening her eyes, she turned to drop her passport on the counter, next to Jake's. 'Can I have a window seat, please?'

Boarding cards in hand, they walked towards the departure lounge.

'I suppose I should be grateful that you're not trying to

impress me by whisking me off in your private plane.' She couldn't resist one small crack.

'I'd be a pretty sad individual if I thought Cassie Travers would be impressed by a private plane,' Jake said wryly. 'Besides which, it's still in the States. I haven't decided yet whether to bring it over.'

Cassie sat on the very edge of the seat, determined not to sink into its luxurïous depths. Her eyes were fixed, looking straight ahead of her. She might be sitting in the First Class lounge, but she *wasn't* going to let the surroundings have any impact on her. If she didn't look, she wouldn't be tempted. It might be childish, but it *was* effective.

A small surge of panic bubbled in her chest. *What are you doing here?* She'd let Jake get her mad and sweep her off her feet. Now that the indignation over Jake trying to steal her investigation was fading, reality was setting in. Benson wasn't her client anymore and it *really* shouldn't matter to her what he was doing.

But she was going to *France*. Abandoning her work and just heading off. On a whim. On the wildest of wild goose chases. *With Jake.*

She was starting to hyperventilate. She had to get her breathing under control before he came back from the men's room. Huh! They probably had geisha girls at the door, handing out hot towels ...

A spurt of laughter conquered the breathlessness. Now *that* was absurd ... And so was her overreaction to Jake. Her physical response was setting her nerves jangling and stopping her from thinking straight. Pure hormonal overdrive. Even now she could walk out of here, if she wanted. But there wasn't any need. She would be away for a few days at most. The business wouldn't fall apart without her. She could work while she was away. She could prove to Jake, and to herself, that whatever had existed between them all those years ago was over, give or take a few misplaced hormones. *The man is a hunk; a girl is allowed a few hormones.*

Hah! For once a little support from the inner voice. A short trip was *not* going to do any harm. And she was going to the *Riviera*. Where Jason's aunt had a home. Where Jason himself might be. How cool was that? She'd be exactly where she needed to be for her best chance of tracking him down. It was practically destiny.

When Jake came back, holding two bone china cups of fresh ground coffee, she greeted him with a smile that made him blink.

'It should be just ahead.' Cassie looked up from the directions provided by the villa rental company and let out a strangled gasp. 'Is that it?'

It was pale pink, with ice-white shutters. And a turret. Jasmine and ivy clung to the walls. It should have looked ridiculous, like a child's toy castle. Under the blue sky, in the shimmering sunshine, it looked impossibly romantic and absurdly pretty.

'Villa Constanza,' Jake confirmed, as he stopped the car. 'That's Verdi, behind us and down the hill.'

They got out. Cassie swung round casually, to examine their quarry. She didn't want to look suspicious, should anyone be watching. She stretched, taking in the scenery, like any newly arrived tourist.

The Villa Verdi was a broad white building, with dark shutters, most of which were closed. It gave the place a faint air of menace. It didn't look as if anyone was at home.

Jake was getting the bags out of the boot. 'The key should be in the envelope that had the directions.'

Cassie had already found it. She held it up. The key looked like something out of a fairy tale too, decorated with curls and spirals. She strode up the steps, put it in the lock and turned.

The door gave onto a large, square hall, with a chessboard floor of black and white tiles. A staircase, with an ornate gilded balustrade, curved upwards. Sunlight spilled in from a domed skylight in the roof. Through an open set of double doors she caught a glimpse of a high-ceilinged room and beyond it French windows, a terrace and the blue glint of a pool. She took all of this in, in one first, breathless sweep.

It was the table set in the middle of the hall that caught and riveted her eyes. White roses, a silver ice bucket, with the unmistakable neck of a champagne bottle protruding from it, two delicate flute glasses, a scattering of confetti and a large notice.

'Congratulations and every happiness in your future life together, Mr and Mrs McQuire,' she read, in a rising squeak.

'Jake!' She turned wrathfully to confront him as he stepped through the door. 'Did you tell these people that we were on our honeymoon?'

Chapter Thirteen

'Honeymoon? Who said anything about a honeymoon? What bee have you got buzzing in your bonnet now, Cass?'

She watched as he did what she had done. A quick glance round, and then homing in on the table, checking where she was pointing.

Then he began to laugh.

He was laughing so much he dropped the bags. Weaving across the hall, he sank down to sit on the stairs, head in hands.

It was just too much. Cassie fought hard, but she couldn't help it. The sound of his laughter was infectious. It was draining all her perfectly righteous indignation, dammit! She was smiling – actually smiling – she could feel her mouth turning up, whether she wanted it to or not. She strode across the hall, stopping in front of him to nudge him with her toe. 'It's not that funny. You really didn't know about this?'

He tipped his head to look up at her. The laughter had drifted into a broad grin. And *that* was doing strange things to her stomach. Things that she didn't want to acknowledge.

'I swear.' He made a heart crossing gesture. 'Trust me, Cass. This had nothing to do with me. It's a misunderstanding.'

He put out his hands to draw her close to him, so her legs were resting against his knees. They eyed each other for a second. Jake's hands were loosely clasped around her, but he wasn't holding her tightly. She could lean in – or step away. For a second the warm air seemed to shimmer. His eyes had gone dark and still and clouded. She lowered her gaze to his mouth. *All you have to do is bend down. You could run your tongue along his lips, taste—*

With a jerk she stepped back, breaking his hold.

'Uh! Wait a minute. If they think we're on our honeymoon—'

She brushed past him and up the stairs, onto the landing, throwing open doors. Bathrooms, a linen closet, rooms where the beds were bare and unmade up.

She should have known straight away it would be *that* door, the one directly ahead of her. She shoved it open and her heart catapulted into her mouth.

It was perfect.

Filmy drapes billowed gently at long open windows, disturbed by the cross draught from the door. The scent of roses came to meet her from blowsy, overfull bowls, dotted about the room, and from climbers planted outside the windows. Fat, white candles waited to be lit. Furniture gleamed and mirrors glittered, but it was the bed that stunned her most. A massive four-poster, with delicate barley-twist columns rising towards a blue ceiling, painted with clouds. Voile hangings, scattered with crystals, floated out from the columns. The bed linen was pure white. Real linen, she noted, with awe. A trail of pink rose petals lay, like an invitation, across the smooth coverlet …

Cassie's chest closed in, as if something was squeezing it. Tears were filming at the edge of her eyelids. It was extravagant, over the top, sheer, complete romance.

But not for you ...

She was barely aware of Jake coming up behind her, until he put his hands on her shoulders.

'Umm.' She felt, rather than heard him let out a long breath. 'Someone went to a lot of trouble.'

Cassie managed a nod. 'Yes.' Her throat was too clogged to manage anything more.

'Don't worry about it, Slick. You have this room. There are plenty of others.' Jake jerked his head to the open door of the linen cupboard on the landing behind them. 'Plenty of bedding too. It won't take long to make up another bed.'

'Two beds.' Cassie stepped back and closed the door. 'That—I don't want to sleep in that room.' *Not alone. And the alternative ...*

'Whatever you prefer.' Jake swivelled round, waving his hand. 'Take your pick. I'll get the bags.'

Cassie emptied the contents of her suitcase onto the bed and gazed at it in horror. She looked at the pile, and then into the bag. She even ran her hand around the inside. Nothing. This was it. Except it couldn't be. She'd thrown things in without much thought, but this couldn't *really* be her packing. Could it?

'Oh no.' She stirred the multi-coloured mound. 'Oh hell!'

The underwear she'd snatched out of the drawer was her newest, most respectable stuff and – thank heavens – her make-up bag was there, plus a handful of sweet-smelling bath and shower goodies from Lush. But her clothes. Where were her clothes?

She sat down on the corner of the bed with a thump, staring at the heap with a disconsolate groan.

This is what happens when you pack a case while the world's most irritating man inspects the books and CDs in your living room.

The filmy, mint-green top that was one of her favourites was there, but not the sexy black Capri pants that went with it. Both the blouses were dark patterned buttoned-to-the-neck, long-sleeved affairs. She hadn't even been wearing them at home for the last month. And she couldn't *believe* she'd stuffed in her fleece. *For early summer, on the Riviera?*

She pounced eagerly on a pair of jeans, dropping them with a small squeak when she saw the paint daubed across the knees. How had that old pair, that she wore for DIY, even got into her wardrobe, much less into her case? She prodded the ragged tangle of denim, chewing her lip. 'Distressed' was a fashion statement, wasn't it? Even some of the big name designers ... *Get real! No one is going to believe those rips and stains were put there by any designer.*

Resisting the temptation to put her head in her hands, she gritted her teeth and began to sort through the unpromising pile. Cramming the impossible stuff back into her case and kicking it as far under the bed as she could manage, she surveyed what she had left.

A heavy wool pencil skirt, the green top and the blouses, a cream linen jacket and the clothes she stood up in. The black blazer and skinny white jeans she was wearing were fine for the cool unpredictability of early summer in Bath. In the warmth of late afternoon on the Riviera she was overheated and sticky. She took off the blazer, and the cotton sweater she had on under it, swapping it for one of the blouses. She looked longingly at the green top, but as her only passable piece of clothing, she'd have to keep that for when she really needed it.

There was a full-length mirror in the en-suite bathroom. The blouse hung loose and was slightly cooler, but she looked staid, fussy and way too formal. She tried rolling up the sleeves and undoing the neck. If anything, that was worse.

Rolling down the sleeves, which were now crumpled, she looked with a shudder at the pair of sturdy lace-up boots she'd managed to pack. The flat black pumps she had on would have to do. She combed her hair, renewed her lipstick, made a face at herself in the mirror and went to find Jake.

She found him at the back of the villa, lounging by the pool. Just looking at him, in a low-slung pair of cut-off jeans and an unbuttoned white shirt, made her feel hot. Hot – as in high temperature. *Yes, well, the other kind of hot too.*

He tipped the ultra black sunglasses down his nose to examine her. 'You're very business-like.'

'Yes, well. Some of us are here to work.' She stared pointedly at the paperback thriller balanced on his midriff, then wished she hadn't, because she had trouble looking away from the long, sleek muscles of his abdomen.

'This *is* work.' He held up a discreet set of binoculars. She hadn't noticed them lying beside him on the steamer chair. *Other things were attracting your attention.* She took them when he offered them to her.

The Villa Verdi leapt at her through powerful lenses. She restrained herself, just in time, from taking an involuntary step back. Bracing her elbows on a convenient balustrade, she ran the glasses slowly over the building. There was no sign of life. Disappointed, she returned the glasses to Jake. Ignoring the jerk of his head which invited her to take the adjacent chair, she sat down stiffly at a wrought iron table. There was a pitcher of water, clinking with ice and garnished with lemon, keeping cool under the shade of an umbrella. She filled a glass and drank gratefully.

'What you think? Is anyone home?'

'If they are, then they're lying low. But they may simply be out.' He looked at his watch. 'Or still at work. We'll have a better idea later. If there's anyone living there, there will be lights,' he explained.

'Mmm.' Cassie chewed her lip. 'I think we need a plan of action and a timetable.' She extracted a small notepad and pen from her pocket. Jake watched with visible amusement as she found a clean page. She ignored his smile. 'What do we know?' She sucked the end of the pen, before writing. 'Villa Verdi, and the restaurant in San Remo – the one on the card from the apartment,' she answered Jake's raised eyebrow. 'Next Monday we'll have dinner in Menton – that's five days away. Before that we need to have thoroughly checked out the Villa, and the other restaurant.'

'And the casino, don't forget that.'

'No.' Cassie shifted uneasily as she added it to her list. She didn't know what the dress code was for Riviera casinos, but she suspected that her meagre wardrobe might have trouble meeting it. *Oh well, you're not going to be seeing anyone you know. And Jake ... Well, it really doesn't matter what Jake thinks.* He was amusing himself by tormenting her, for some peculiar reason of his own. That was his problem, not hers. She was here to find out what Benson was up to. And maybe track down Jason? She'd forgotten to bring the list of gardens out of her 'Fairbook' file. She made a note on a new page, to ask Benita to find it.

'We could go down now and have a closer look at the Villa Verdi.' She closed the notebook.

'I think we need to find out a little more, before we start poking around.' Jake clasped his hands behind his head. 'It might look deserted, but there could still be a Doberman the size of a tank fast asleep behind the house. And if there is someone at home – as you said this morning, we can't just pitch up any-old-how, asking questions about Benson.'

Restlessly Cassie got to her feet. 'Okay – we need information. Any suggestions on how we get it?'

'We give a party.'

Surprised, Cassie sat down again with a thump. 'A party?'

'We invite all the neighbours round for drinks,' Jake explained. 'Let them get a good look at us, to establish how innocent and above board we are, and give us a chance for a good look at them.'

Cassie examined the idea. She had to admit it sounded promising. It would have sounded even better if most of her wardrobe wasn't still in Bath. With a pang of longing for a stunning little vintage cocktail dress that she hadn't worn yet, she nodded. 'What if the Villa Verdi people don't come?'

'We pump the neighbours – discreetly of course. Everyone loves to gossip.'

'We need a cover story – to explain why we're here.'

'We've already got one. Honeymoon?' he prompted, when she stared blankly.

'You said—'

'I promised it was a mistake.' He held up his hand. 'Doesn't mean we can't take advantage of it.'

Cassie was still suspicious. 'If we're on our honeymoon, would we want to be inviting other people around?'

'We're unusual honeymooners – the social kind. Of course, it wouldn't hurt if you could gaze soulfully into my eyes, cling to my arm, laugh at my jokes—'

'In your dreams, McQuire.' Reluctantly, Cassie found herself warming to the idea. It really was quite clever. *Not that you will be telling Jake that.* 'When are we going to have this soiree?'

'How about tomorrow? The management people from the villa will set it all up.'

Cassie inhaled deeply. It was another world, this one Jake inhabited. You simply snapped your fingers and everything happened.

'It's what they do, Cass.' Jake had correctly interpreted her expression.

'I know. It's what I do too. It's just …' *It's just a weird feeling to be on the receiving end.* Her own business provided services for people who could probably do it for themselves, if they had time and inclination. She couldn't knock it. But if you were giving a party … Racing round the supermarket to assemble a trolley full of wine and beer and crisps, cooking pizza and sausage rolls, inviting the whole neighbourhood – that was a big part of the fun. *Different worlds.*

Cassie took another drink from the pitcher of water, then went to explore the rest of the villa. It was cooler inside.

She was impressed with what she found. There was a book-lined study on one side of the hall, with a fine selection of new paperbacks and glossy magazines and a window seat, built into the turret. A small, red-walled dining room overlooked the front of the building, with the kitchen beyond it, down a narrow corridor. A high-tech home cinema and games room and an expensively equipped mini gym occupied the basement.

The main salon stretched almost the breadth of the back of the house. Tall windows gave onto a paved and rose smothered terrace. Another terrace, one shallow step lower, contained the swimming pool. It was a perfect venue for a civilised drinks party. Cassie could picture herself moving from group to group, talking, laughing, offering delicious things to eat, exchanging glances with Jake ...

And all of this, of course, in your good wool skirt and dark green blouse.

Daydream hitting the floor – *and the best place for it, if it involves sharing anything with Jake, even a glance* – she shrugged, and carried on exploring.

She paused in the bedroom she'd chosen, to tie her hair up, so that it didn't press so heavy and hot against her neck. Checking in the mirror on the effect of improvising with a lace from one of her boots, she caught sight of her hands. Her bare hands. Ah! Jake's rings were in the bottom of her handbag. She'd tossed them there, intending to return them, but if they were meant to be married …

She scrabbled in her bag. Locating them at last, she slid them on. The stones caught the sunlight.

Who would guess they're not real?

She dumped the bag on the bed and headed for the door. Her stomach was beginning to grumble. Somewhere in all this luxury there had to be some food.

The kitchen, which seemed to be larger than her whole flat, was over the top state-of-the-art. Pale wood units, granite and marble surfaces, a coffee machine that looked as if it had fallen off the back of a flight deck. Cassie could only guess the purpose of half the electronic gadgets sitting on the work surfaces. Steering well clear of them she wandered around, poking into cupboards and examining the contents of the wine rack. There was an informal dining area as well as a breakfast bar. She found the freezer in a utility room, off to the side. It was easily big enough to stash a dead body.

So, if you really *annoy me, McQuire …*

She stuck her head in the fridge and rummaged – milk, eggs, butter, smoked salmon, salad leaves, three kinds of cheese, Parma ham, melon, raspberries and strawberries, cream, a slab of dark chocolate, two bottles of white wine, more champagne. A bread crock on the floor contained a French stick and a round flat loaf, covered with crystallised salt and herbs. She sniffed cautiously. It smelled delicious. Her mouth watered. Tomatoes stood in a pottery dish. A string of onions, and another of garlic, hung from a brass hook beside the stove.

She was opening drawers and cupboards, finding plates

and cutlery and wondering what she might put together for dinner, when she heard Jake's step behind her. 'Are you hungry?' she asked, without turning. 'Because I am.'

'Good. We'll go down to San Remo, to that restaurant that was on the card in Benson's apartment.' He was looking at his watch as she shut the cupboard door and turned towards him. 'I'll give you ten minutes, if you want to change.'

He had. The blue shirt and close-fitting jeans pulled her breath in, just a little. He looked like the boy she'd know all those years ago. She recollected herself quickly. *This is the big bad wolf who eats city traders for breakfast. Every beat of his heart spells money.*

'I don't need ten minutes. I'll just get my bag and we can go.' She brushed past him, seeing the surprise on his face. 'Come on. I want my dinner.'

Chapter Fourteen

The restaurant was in the middle of town. Wide glass doors stood open to the sultry evening. A cluster of tables, each with a squat red candle burning on it, spilled into the street. More than half were already occupied. There was a delicious aroma of garlic and herbs.

Once they'd given their order Cassie leaned back in her seat and looked around her. She had to be alert to anything that might be a clue to the Benson mystery.

It was a little disappointing.

She and Jake seemed to be the only tourists. Everyone else looked as if they belonged here. A family with two immaculately behaved children and a baby in a high chair occupied a corner. An elderly couple sampled mouthfuls of food from each other's plates. A much younger couple held hands across the table.

Suddenly, alarmingly, Cassie's stomach gave a deep lurch of longing. *She* wanted to belong, to be with someone she could grow old with, whose hand she could hold, in the romantic semi-dark. Her fingers stretched out to Jake, of their own volition. She pulled them back and folded them in her lap. She was strong, independent and in control. She could do without romance. She certainly didn't need that sort of dangerous thought anywhere around Jake. *Lust – now that is an entirely different matter*.

He was lounging in his chair, scanning the restaurant as she had done. He looked sleek and relaxed, but she wasn't fooled. She looked down at his hands, long and capable, capable of—

'Why are you here, Jake?'

He looked startled. 'I thought we were here to sleuth? What'd you think about that couple over there? Suspicious or what?'

Involuntarily Cassie turned her head, and bit her lip down on a giggle. The table Jake indicated was occupied by the most respectable looking pair she'd ever seen; stolid, middle-aged, comfortable. *Not like the damn pirate sitting across from you.*

'We really have no idea what we're looking for, do we?' She sighed and picked out a gleaming black olive from the dish the waiter had brought.

'I expect it's like art – we'll know it when we see it. And I don't think there's anyone here tonight to interest us.' Jake was rummaging in the olives, picking them up two at a time. 'Lunchtime might be better – they probably get a lot of business types.'

Their food arrived. Cassie concentrated on her plate of pasta, careful to make sure that her napkin covered her properly. She couldn't afford even a speck of spaghetti sauce in her lap.

Jake watched Cassie eat. It was no hardship; he could watch her mouth for hours. He frowned slightly. She'd been curiously jumpy since they'd arrived, and he didn't think it was down to sharing the Villa Constanza with him – at least not all of it. The honeymoon cock-up could have wrecked *everything*. Heads would roll over that, he promised himself darkly. Jake McQuire didn't pay for screw-ups. She'd taken his word on it, thankfully. *Which is weird, as she distrusts most everything else you say.*

Looking at her now, swathed in the generous napkin that the restaurant provided, an unfamiliar sense of confusion washed over him. That question from her, that he'd sidestepped, came slithering back into his brain. *Why are you here?* Same question, but not the way she meant it. Not that he really knew what Cassie meant by it either. Women were a mystery. Sure, he was sitting in a restaurant with a beautiful example of the species, but one who was spitting and scratching and downright awkward most of the time. Right now, with all those folds of linen draped over her, she looked like a little kid protecting her best party frock. It wasn't as if the outfit she had on was anything special. The blouse was some dull, plain, heavy fabric. Was this a new game plan – dress ugly, so he wouldn't fancy her? *I have news for you, Ms Travers. It ain't working.*

He dug his hand into his hair. That pulse of desire was always there between them, like background music. And he was pretty damn sure he wasn't playing solo here. It wouldn't take more than a spark to get the whole volcano thing rocking again. If he made that push, Cassie would be his. This he *knew.* But that wasn't the deal. He'd set all this up, taken extraordinary care with it, and it was working out just as he wanted. The villa, this restaurant – the setting was relaxing, romantic but subtle. Anything more, and …

He felt his lip twitching into a reluctant smile. Anything more and he could almost see Cassie making pass-me-the-sick-bag gestures. *Then* she'd try to knee him in the groin.

An abrupt wave of irritation constricted his chest and he reached for a slug of wine. He was waiting. Something was supposed to happen next. So – what was it? *You don't have a clue.*

It all came back to a single conversation – with another woman he didn't understand. His mother. A conversation that had ended in a bet, but that they'd never really finished. Not to his satisfaction. Heaven knows, he'd tried. Raised the subject a dozen times. No dice. Even when he'd finally been goaded enough to ask her, straight out, the night before she left. *Define what the end game is.*

Ma had only grinned, and carried on packing. He didn't know what came next, and it bugged the hell out of him. He was just *here*, feeling his way in the dark. It caught him off balance, and that was *not* where he liked to be. He dug his fork into his pasta, wondering if he was ever going to figure it out. Then Cassie looked up and smiled a *really* evil smile.

'Don't think you're off the hook, McQuire, just because I'm hungry and this is good.' She chewed appreciatively. 'Why are you here?'

'Sleuthing – and the pleasure of your company.' *Get back on track, McQuire.*

'You're hoping to get me into bed.'

'Cass, there's not a guy between the ages of sixteen and ninety who would look at you and *not* think about getting you into bed.' He caught a dangling strand of spaghetti off his fork and sucked it up. 'I'm simply a poor SoB, like all the others.' He treated her to his most lascivious grin. 'I'm just hoping to be a *luckier* SoB.'

* * *

In the romantic dimness of the restaurant, Cassie's cheeks heated. How did he *do* that? Pay her a compliment, of sorts, then pull the rug out from under her, all at the same time! She harrumphed into her pasta. Jake reached over and tapped her hand lightly. She dropped her fork and it took three tries to pick it up.

'We have issues, Slick. Want to talk them through?'

'No.'

'Rii-ight. So, if you don't want to talk about *us*, how about telling me about the guy who hosed you—conned you,' he translated.

'Benita has a big mouth.'

Jake shook his head. 'Bennie is worried about you, and her job, but it wasn't her. Tony told me.'

'Then *Tony* has a big mouth.' Cassie narrowed her eyes. 'I'd forgotten you two had reinstated the lads' night in – what is it these days? Beer and pizza and porn movies?' She opened her eyes wide, suddenly inspired. '*Don't* tell me you still put on those old heavy metal tracks and play air guitar?' The trace of a flush on his cheekbones had her crowing. 'You do! You do!'

'Yeah, alright, we did. *Once*. One. Time.' He held up a finger to illustrate. 'Those tracks aren't *old*, they're vintage.'

Cassie was still spluttering into her wine glass. Jake nudged her under the table with his foot. 'Come on. I told you my deadly secret – you tell me yours. What about this guy Jason?'

'If that's the deadliest secret you have in your cupboards, McQuire, then I'll eat that pepper-pot.' Cassie gestured to the gigantic wooden mill on the table between them. 'Why are you so interested in my disasters anyway? The rat took my money. End of story.'

'Not quite. Tony said you were trying to find him?'

'To get the cash back, yeah.'

'So, tell me,' Jake urged. 'Maybe I can help.' He shook his head when Cassie grimaced. 'It's not impossible, Slick. We're here, working together, aren't we?'

'Yes.' Cassie shrugged. 'Okay. His name is Jason Fairbrook. When I met him – he … he seemed such a nice guy. *My* sort of guy. Gentle, kind, funny. *Not* like you, McQuire. Well, I guess you *can* be funny. Sometimes.'

Jake dipped his head, in sardonic acknowledgement. 'Gee, thanks.'

Cassie favoured him with a quick sneer. It bounced off, but he *was* listening. 'I was teaching Jason the business. He was talking about doing the butler training, so he could help out when we needed it. I intended for us to be partners. I really thought, this time …'

She stopped, voice thickening. The waiter had taken her plate, but on Jake's advice she'd kept hold of her cutlery. She used the fork to draw a pattern on the tablecloth. The image of Jason, as she'd first seen him, drifted in her mind. Tall, blond, diffident, with that lovely slow, slightly dopey smile. She'd just *known* that he had so much potential, and she had so much to give.

Jake, watching her down bent head, had a sudden desire to dig slimebag Jason's heart out of his chest, with a blunt knife. The strength of the emotion rocked him for a second. Then Cassie looked up, and the feeling faded into something completely different at the sight of the confusion in her eyes.

* * *

Cassie swallowed. How foolish she'd been. 'Jason had the keys to the office, of course – and the safe. Bennie had just sent out a batch of invoices.' She paused and sipped her wine. It felt cool on her tongue. This was the hardest part to admit – the part that hurt. 'I found out later that Jason had offered discounts for payment in cash. When I walked into the office on Monday morning the safe was open and empty. Jason was supposed to have banked the money on Friday, but there was no paperwork. Then, when he didn't turn up at the office ...'

She shifted in her seat, remembering her disbelief, followed by the increasingly frantic phone calls – to Jason's landlady, to the bank, to friends. She'd even rung the gym he'd used. 'He'd just disappeared. Given notice at his lodging, even sold his car.'

Jake topped up their glasses. 'Police?'

Cassie shook her head. 'I didn't want ...' She shrugged. 'When it came down to it, I'd *given* him the keys.' She straightened her shoulders as the waiter put a crisp-fried fillet of fish down in front of her. 'Jason couldn't have just vanished into thin air.' She heard her voice harden. 'He must have left a trail. I've been piecing together what I can remember – what I've found out. He has an aunt he was close to. She has a house here, somewhere on the Riviera.'

'Then we add that to your list of things to investigate,' Jake said matter-of-factly, gesturing with his fork. 'Now eat, before it gets cold and the chef throws a tantrum – and the carving knife.'

Cassie declined dessert, in favour of an espresso, but let Jake feed her a spoonful of his tiramisu. 'You still have a

104

sweet tooth.' She refused another spoonful with a wave of her hand. 'I haven't forgotten that time you tried to get a whole chocolate bar in your mouth, and nearly choked.'

'Can't say I've attempted that trick lately.'

Cassie sighed reminiscently. 'We did a lot of very stupid things when we were young.'

'That's what being young is all about. There were a lot of good things too.' He reached out and ran his finger, very lightly, across her knuckles. Cassie suppressed a shiver.

'Don't go all gooey on me, McQuire. The past is the past. You're not softening me up that way.'

Jake's wide-eyed would-I-do-that stare didn't fool her. He tilted his head. 'I did say we had issues that we should talk about.'

'The only issue we have is finding Benson. And Jason, if you're serious about helping me with that.'

'Do you doubt me, Slick? I'm heartbroken.'

'I doubt *everything* about you, Mister,' she responded cheerfully. 'Are you ready to go?'

They paid the bill and Cassie pocketed it, to add to the account she was keeping of her expenses.

They were leaving the restaurant, threading their way through the tables, when the disaster happened.

Chapter Fifteen

Cassie didn't see it coming. One of the children from the party at the front of the restaurant, returning from the washroom, squeezed past her, with a polite murmur. Maybe she stepped forward too quickly, after letting the child through. Maybe the child accidentally pulled the corner of the tablecloth, in passing. Maybe the man at the table simply fumbled with his glass. The first thing she knew, it was in motion, spilling straight towards her. The second was when the wine hit, splashing out in a wide red arc, before the glass shattered on the floor.

Everyone was talking at once. Two waiters rushed over, one to offer towels and mop up, the other to retrieve the glass shards. The man at the table and the child's mother were loud and concerned in their apologies. Cassie stood, frozen, the wine soaking into her white jeans. *What the hell are you going to wear in the morning?*

'You okay, Slick?' Jake was frowning at her no doubt dazed expression.

'Yeah.' She unclenched her jaw. 'It's cool. No one got hurt.' Nodding her thanks to the waiters, she grabbed Jake's arm. 'Can we just get out of here, please?'

When they reached the villa, Cassie was out of the car and haring inside as soon as it came to rest. Jake followed more slowly. Hearing doors slam and Cassie's footsteps echoing overhead, accompanied by a muffled string of curses, he changed direction. Heading into the salon, he poured himself a small measure of brandy and took it out onto the terrace. Sipping slowly, he stepped down to the lower level. Warm, dark air enveloped him, heavy with the scent of jasmine and lightly spiced with a trace of chlorine.

He stopped when he reached the edge of the pool. The water gleamed turquoise, lit from beneath. The hint of a breeze carried snatches of music from one of the nearby villas – opera – a mournful tenor crooning about lost love. Jake let out a long breath. He hadn't smoked for at least five years, but right now he could use a cigarette. He rocked his foot against the edge of the pool.

One glass of red wine can sure break up a mood.

He knocked back the brandy, extinguished the outside lamps and went inside, paying no attention at all to the lights that burned brightly from the windows of the Villa Verdi.

'Do not trouble yourself any more this morning, Signora. I will see what can be done.' Vitoria, the maid, who had arrived with the morning's breakfast, surveyed Cassie's ravaged blouse and jeans with a sympathetic eye.

'Is there anything?' Cassie frowned doubtfully. The marks had started to dry before she could deal with them. She'd worked every stain removing trick she knew, washing out most of the wine, but there was still a fine tracery of disfiguring pink splotches on the white jeans.

'I will take them to la mia mamma, my mother. If it can be fixed, she will know.' Vitoria rolled up the offending garments with a smile. 'Now – I have laid the table on the terrace beside the pool. The Signore, he is already there.'

She ushered Cassie towards the door. 'I will bring fresh coffee, presto.'

'Mille grazie.'

'Prego.'

As Cassie stepped outside, warmth hit her like a wall. Her heart sank to around her knees, and kept on going. Dressed as she was, in the remaining blouse and heavy skirt, she'd hoped that the morning, at least, would be cool. Black wool lovingly enveloped her legs, drawing the warmth of the sun. Dampness was already collecting at the back of the dark blue blouse. She plodded over to the table.

Jake, disgustingly cool in a pale blue shirt and casual cream chinos, looked up from his copy of the Wall Street Journal. Cassie saw the surprise register in his eyes. 'Good morning.' Casually he pushed a jug of orange juice towards her, then hefted the coffee pot. 'I think this is empty.'

'It's all right, Vitoria is bringing more.' Cassie knew her face must be pink. It was certainly uncomfortably clammy. It was all she could do to stop herself wrenching at the neck of the blouse, to give herself some air, even here in the shade. Jake was regarding her quizzically over the juice.

'Yes. I am warm. All right?' she admitted, goaded. 'I ... didn't expect it to be so hot here,' she improvised. *It's not entirely a lie.*

'You mean that everything you have—' He paused to give the blouse and skirt a quick once over.

'Yes.'

'I see.' His head was slanted. There was the suggestion of a grin.

Oh, yes, it's all very funny. Cassie lowered her eyes to

the jug of orange juice and kept them fixed there. Cool trails of condensation were running down its sides. She almost snatched at a glass, filled it and drank gratefully.

Jake pushed a basket of bread and pastries towards her. 'You'd better finish your breakfast as fast as possible, before you melt.' When her head jerked up, he treated her to a wide smile. 'Then we'll hit the shops.'

'Jake McQuire, I am *not* letting you buy me clothes.' They stood on the narrow pavement in front of a shop window with a delectable selection of summer outfits. They looked so good Cassie wanted to eat them. Just standing and staring was taking some of the heat out of her flushed face.

'Cass—'

'This is not *Pretty Woman*. You are not doing that Richard Gere thing.'

'D'you know, I never saw that movie,' Jake responded blandly.

Cassie pursed her lips in frustration. Heat, panic and longing struggled in her chest. How was she expected to keep a cool head to track down Benson and Jason, when her system was in meltdown – *and this time it has nothing to do with Jake's sex appeal.*

As if making a point, a trickle of perspiration stung the corner of her eye.

Her will-power collapsed abruptly. 'One outfit, maybe two. And everything you lend me will be just that – a loan.'

'Whatever.' He held out a slim silver card. 'Go on. Take it.' His grin was in danger of splitting his face. 'Do damage. Hit me where it hurts – in the wallet.'

Cassie hesitated. 'Would it?'

'Nah.' He pressed the card into her palm. 'I doubt if you'll even dent it, Slick. And remember, you do have Benson's money to pay me back.'

'I'm not touching that!' With her brain scrambling in the heat, the denial came out a lot more vehemently than it should.

'Ploughing it back into the business. Very wise.' The compliment was spoiled by the way Jake was still grinning. 'Tell you what – if using my card really bothers you so much, how about you do a little contract work for Kings – helping out when we need it, to pay off what you borrow?'

'What sort of helping out?'

'Oh, I don't know. This and that. I'm sure we'll find something.'

Yes, I'm sure you will too.

Her fingers had folded themselves around the card. If she agreed to work for the detective agency, she'd still be tied to Jake when this was over.

Oh, what the hell.

'Okay, it's a deal.' She lifted her chin. 'And if I'm going to do this, then I might as well enjoy it.'

She tossed her hair back, opened the door of the shop and stalked inside.

Amused at the novelty of having to force his credit card on a woman, Jake ambled after her, watching her legs. Cassie had an excellent pair of pins. Even swathed in black wool, they looked damn good.

Chapter Sixteen

'I don't think I've ever spent quite so much money quite so fast.' After a hectic half-hour, they were back in the street, surrounded by carrier bags. Cassie was wearing a pale lemon camisole and a full white skirt. She was a hundred degrees cooler and a little dizzy. 'Can we sit down for minute, and have an iced coffee?'

Jake was behind her. She turned her head. His attention was clearly elsewhere. She followed his gaze. Into another shop window.

It was a dress. White, but splashed all over with swathes of vivid colour. Eye- grabbing, feminine, sexy.

That garment is lethally expensive. Get the hell away from here.

Even as the thought came, her heartbeat accelerated. She wasn't salivating, but it was close. She turned her head away quickly but not quickly enough. Jake had seen the flash of hunger in her eyes. *Dammit.*

'Slick, that dress has your name on it. You *have* to try it on.'

'No.' She backed away, almost falling over the heap of bags.

'Yes.' He took her arm and pulled her forward. 'You need something for the party tonight, and to wear to the casino. *That* is it.'

Cassie dug in her heels. She'd just caught sight of the discreet price label, displayed beside the mannequin. It was worse than she'd even *imagined*. 'I'd be working for you *forever* to pay that off.'

'Slave labour.' His voice was dark with laughter. 'Why didn't I think of it before? You *have* to have that dress. Don't worry.' His eyes glittered. 'I'm sure I can think of a creative way for you to pay off the debt more quickly.'

Something tightened in the pit of Cassie's stomach. *What is the matter with you?* She should be fighting not to be beholden to Jake. Instead there was an unbelievable feeling of – excitement? He was teasing. She knew he was teasing, and yet—

'No!'

'Yes!' He bent to gather the bags, one-handed, still with his grip on her elbow. 'Come on. It's not that bad, the price on the label is in euros, remember.' He was towing her gently towards the shop and her legs were refusing to run in the other direction. 'Look on the bright side – maybe it won't fit.'

It did fit.

When Cassie saw her reflection in the mirror, followed by the expression on Jake's face, as she walked out of the changing cubicle, she knew she was lost.

Even if she had to work for Jake for the rest of her life. Even if she had to—

Well, maybe not *that* ...

The sales woman had swathes of tissue paper and a box waiting when Cassie re-emerged from the cubicle, dressed in the lemon and white outfit. She handed over the dress. The sales woman clucked lovingly over it. Jake was leaning against the counter.

'I've been thinking.'

'Yes? Why does this worry me?'

'Because you're a natural worrier?'

'I have awards for it. Go on then.' She folded her arms. 'Hit me with it, straight out.'

'Of course, I know nothing about these things.' He'd cast his eyes up, in an effort to look innocent. It was *so* not working. 'But what about underneath—'

'If you mean underwear, McQuire, then say so.'

'That's the stuff,' he agreed.

'Taken care of. I have no needs in that direction.'

'Uh.' He didn't attempt to keep the disappointment out of his tone. Cassie just about stopped her lip quivering. It took a *lot* of effort. Undeterred, he looked her up and down, stopping at her feet and the sensible black pumps. 'Ah – shoes.'

'No, Jake. No, No, No.'

'Cass, you can't come to Italy and not buy shoes.'

The car was parked in the shade of an archway. They stashed a mountain of carrier bags, along with cheese, fruit and thick slabs of olive-studded bread on the back seat and in the boot. Cassie tried not to tremble when she thought of the lusciously beaded evening shoes; the kitten-heeled courts in soft, nude leather; the red and white striped espadrilles; the silver sandals ... Not to mention the deliciously multi-strapped affairs in pale yellow that she was wearing. *Working for Jake, forever.*

'Coffee? At the place opposite where we ate last night?' Jake suggested. 'Check it out in daylight?'

'What do you think?' Cassie licked froth off her cappuccino spoon. Jake's eyes flickered. Cassie put the bowl of the spoon in her mouth and sucked.

'As you undoubtedly realise, I'm not thinking at all. You've totally taken my mind off the reason we're here.'

'You always did have a short attention span.'

Jake's eyes were hot on her face. 'Cass, I assure you that for some things I can summon up a great deal of attention. For a *very* long time.'

Cassie shivered. She'd asked for that. What was the attraction of playing with fire? A sensation of Jake's mouth, hard on hers, floated into her brain. She shut down on it, fast.

'Sorry.' She looked away. 'There are two men, sitting on the left. One of them is English. There's a logo on his bag. Might be a sports club.' She took out the notebook and scribbled in it.

'What about that woman—hello, she's on the move.'

A dark woman, wearing opaque wrap-around shades, rose from her seat at the bar and approached the men's table. She put her hand on logo-man's shoulder, spoke briefly and pressed a paper into his hand. Cassie quickly closed the book, to cover her notes and drawings, as the woman left the restaurant, crossing the street and walking past them.

She frowned. 'Do you think they're anything to do with Benson?'

'Hard to say. Could just be a hooker, touting for business.'

'You have a low, cynical mind.'

'Thank you.' Jake nodded and gestured for the bill.

Back at the villa a note from Vitoria announced that caterers would be arriving at four, with cocktails and canapés, and that fifteen of the neighbours had accepted the invitation.

'But are the occupants of the Villa Verdi amongst them?' Cassie speculated. The house was still shuttered, and apparently deserted. 'Did you see any lights last night?'

Jake shrugged. They were sitting beside the pool, under the enormous umbrella. The remnants of a leisurely lunch, of cheese, tomatoes and the olive bread, lay on the table. Cassie raised her eyebrows in the direction of Jake's laptop, moved out of reach of crumbs and splashes. Obligingly he pushed it towards her.

'I'm going to type Benson's name, coupled with the Villa Verdi, into a few search engines, see if anything comes up. Don't know why I didn't think of it sooner.'

'Already done.' Jake typed a few lines of text, pushed some keys and clicked on a link. He turned the device to show her the page.

'Mmm. Nothing really useful.' She wrinkled her nose. 'It looks like Gerald Benson *could* be an alias,' she noted, as she scrolled.

'I'd say I was certain of it.' Jake got up and stretched. 'Swim?'

'Maybe, later.' When she'd figured out whether any of her underwear would double as a bikini. 'I'll see what I can find about the logo on the man's bag.'

Jake nodded, slid off the shirt he was wearing over his trunks and dived into the pool. Cassie rearranged the machine, so that she wouldn't be tempted to watch as he powered through the water, then let out a frustrated sigh when she realised her notebook, with the drawing of the logo, was upstairs in her bag.

She'd just pushed back her chair, on her way to retrieve it, when Jake loomed beside her, dripping like a sea god, newly risen from the waves. He reached for a towel. Sea god ... that was exactly how he looked, with shining water droplets running down sleek smooth muscles. She swallowed hard. 'Not a very long swim.'

'Enough.' He shook his head, rubbing vigorously at his hair. Cassie tried not to watch. 'We can't stay out here too much longer, the caterers will be arriving soon, to set up. It's too lovely to stay indoors. How about a drive?'

'I ...' Cassie made a half-hearted gesture towards the computer. 'I should be working, or finding out more about Benson.' She was having trouble keeping her eyes off Jake's chest, his arms, his legs ...

'Why not wait until after the party? You can follow up anything useful then.'

There was a strange tension in the air. With an abrupt movement Jake hooked a robe from the back of a chair. Cassie let out her breath in a long sigh as he shrugged himself into it. He picked up his watch from the table, frowning down at it. 'We really don't have long before it will be time to get ready.' He looked up again, head tilted. 'But enough time for a trip to the ice-cream parlour.'

'Ice-cream parlour?'

'We passed it on the way home. You didn't see it?'

Cassie shook her head. She hesitated, looking at the laptop, then she leaned over and shut the lid with a snap.

'What are we waiting for?' She shooed him towards the house. 'Go and get dressed.'

Chapter Seventeen

The soft sound of voices and the clinking of bottles floated upwards, on the warm evening air. Cassie leaned over the balcony of her room, attracted by the sound of the preparations below. On the terrace the caterers had set up the bar. Ice buckets and glasses sparkled invitingly. Pots of hot-house flowers were dotted over the steps and around the pool, interspersed with miniature orange and lemon trees. Festoons of tiny white lights swathed the balustrades and hung from obelisks. A string quartet was tuning up in the shade of a pergola.

'Come on down, Juliet.' Jake appeared below, like the Demon King, stage left. 'Our guests will be here in a minute.'

'Looking good, Slick.' Jake inspected her with approval as she stepped through the French doors. The dress, *the* dress, swirled softly around her calves. The glint in his eye was decidedly smug. 'Told you those shoes were the finishing touch.'

Cassie examined her feet. Jake could be as smug as he liked. Tonight she didn't care. Delicate silver straps wound from her toes to her ankles. They looked fabulous. They felt fabulous.

Just forget that you'll be paying for this until doomsday.

'Not so bad yourself.' Cassie nodded at his cream suit and dark shirt, then stared beyond him, to where the caterers were opening bottles, slicing fruit and arranging canapés on silver trays. 'This is quite up-market for a casual drinks party.'

'You think so?' Jake looked around, clearly surprised.

'Subtle but classy.'

'Wow! I've impressed you at last.' Before Cassie knew what he was doing, Jake took her hand and raised it to his lips. 'I hope you enjoy every minute of it, darling.'

Cassie was afraid her arm was going into spasm. The light touch of Jake's mouth on the back of her hand had all her nerves fighting – to get to that one warm spot where his lips had touched.

'Well now, Marty, isn't that just *so* romantic?'

Cassie swung round, to see the first of their guests bearing down on them.

Jake leaned close to whisper, his eyes brimming with laughter, 'We're on our honeymoon, remember?'

A waiter was approaching with a tray of champagne. Jake took a glass and presented it to her, before turning back smoothly to greet the first arrivals. 'Hi there. So glad you could make it.'

Cassie stood for moment, eyes shut, letting the tiny pastry case melt on her tongue, and analysing the taste. Salmon mousse and prawns. Totally delicious. *Will the caterer part with the recipe?* When she opened her eyes Jake was standing in front of her. He offered her a fresh drink. It was dark pink and bubbly. When she sipped, it tasted heavenly. She held up the glass to inspect it. 'What is this stuff?'

'Kir Royale. Champagne mixed with cassis.'

Cassie took another greedy mouthful, nodding. 'We've

served it at events. It tasted good, but never like this. I suppose it's the quality of the champagne.' She tightened her hold on the delightfully fizzing glass.

'Possibly.' Jake regarded her with amusement. 'Slick, I do believe you're enjoying yourself.'

'Where is it written down that I can't?'

'Nowhere.' He gave a slight nod. 'There are a couple of newcomers over there that you haven't spoken to yet.'

'I'm on it.' Cassie raised her glass to him and sashayed away, hoping he was watching. She felt relaxed and sort of breathless, all at the same time. She might have had a sip too much champagne. Or maybe it was the dress and the music and the scent of roses and jasmine?

It was probably the champagne.

She was disappointed that no one from the Villa Verdi had turned up, but she'd gleaned some information. The language barrier had been no problem. Several of their neighbours were ex-pats and fellow rentals, and most of the others spoke some English. Plus Jake's Italian sounded pretty fluent to her. *Huh! You have definitely had too much to drink, if you're letting Jake impress you. He can't be that good, or he'd have been able to translate that stuff on the answer-phone.*

Getting back to business, she introduced herself to the newcomers, and soon found herself part of a small chattering group.

'You know what I heard this afternoon?' A man with a bright red shirt and designer stubble drained his glass and helped himself to another.

'Madonna is buying that house near the Russian church.' A woman in a slim white dress was taking her time choosing canapés from the tray of a particularly good-looking waiter.

'Is she?' Cassie asked, intrigued.

'Come on—' Red-shirt's partner, a vivacious brunette, giggled. 'Every time someone sells a big property, the rumour goes round that Madonna is buying it.'

Her husband, partner, whatever, grinned triumphantly 'No, not that. I meant about the film.'

He'd got the attention of the woman in the white dress. She took two canapés and dismissed the waiter. 'What film?'

'I heard that too.' A grey-haired man in crumpled linen waved a lighted cigarette. 'They're going to be shooting a film here, in San Remo. Keira Knightley is in it – and that chap from *Lord of the Rings*.'

'I heard it was Kate Winslet and Ralph Fiennes.'

Cassie sipped her drink and joined in the laughter as a few other names were tossed into the mix.

'If it's Hugh Jackman, then I'm definitely first in the queue if they want extras.'

'Darling, we'll *all* be in the queue, but I believe they're called background artistes these days.'

Jake had left the group he was with, moving behind Cassie to greet a latecomer. Cassie turned casually to watch, and caught her breath.

Jake was holding out his hand to the man they'd seen in the restaurant that morning. Logo man.

Chapter Eighteen

'At last!' Before Cassie could move, the Hugh Jackman fan, a tall blonde with diamond tennis bracelets on each wrist, slipped past her, to wrap her arms around Logo man. 'Cassie—' She grinned. 'Meet my *late* husband.'

'Hi.' He stuck out his hand. Bemused, Cassie took it. 'I'm Mitch – thanks for entertaining my wife.' He gave the blonde a peck on the cheek. 'Sorry not to get here sooner. Business.'

'That's what you always say.' His wife wrinkled her nose and punched his arm.

'Truth. I swear.' He accepted a drink from Jake. 'As a matter of fact ... I know this is a bit of a cheek, seeing as I've only just got here, but could we have a word, d'you think?'

Jake gestured towards the open doors to the salon. Cassie flashed him a quick glance. He shrugged and raised his eyebrows as he passed.

'Men!' Mitch's wife gazed after her husband in amused exasperation. 'You'll have to excuse him.' She looked apologetically at Cassie. 'I am trying to domesticate him, but I'm not doing very well.'

Cassie smiled at her woebegone expression. 'I know exactly what you mean.'

The terrace was quiet. The last of the guests had departed and the caterers were ferrying equipment to the front of the villa, loading their van. Cassie leaned on a balustrade, watching the Villa Verdi. Jake stood behind her, inhaling her scent. Sunlight and lemons. Very gently he ran the tip of one finger along her shoulder. The skin was smooth and warm. He reached the thin strap of the white dress. He could just push it away …

Cassie swung round, breaking the contact and scrubbing at her shoulder. 'I think the insects are starting to come out. It felt like something was crawling on me.'

Jake sighed. 'Do you want to go to dinner?'

'Nope. Too full of party food at the moment. Maybe later.'

'In that case, there's something I've wanted to do all evening.'

He scooped her into his arms, and dived for her mouth. She tasted deliciously of blackcurrants and champagne. Caught unawares, she melted into his arms. Her lips softened. She was responding to him. There was even a breathless little moan. *When she gets her wits back, you'll probably pay for this.*

Who cares?

He tightened his hold. Blood was thundering out of his brain. Other parts of his body seemed to think they needed it more. His head swirled as everything started to samba south.

'I want you.' It came out hoarse.

'I know, but *I want* doesn't *get*.' With a sudden wrench, she twisted out of his hold and backed away, coming up against the balustrade. Her breathing was shallow and her face had an intoxicating flush. Despite the prim rebuttal, there was no mistaking the arousal in her eyes. *There are two people in this samba. Her mind might not want you, but her body has other ideas.*

122

He watched appreciatively as her chest rose and fell. She was hauling in deep breaths now, trying to calm herself. She'd summoned up a frown. He wanted to stroke it away – better still, kiss it away.

'We should be discussing the party.' Her voice had a delightful little wobble. 'Comparing notes.' She gestured to the table and two chairs set either side of it.

'We could do that horizontal.' Jake let his frustration show. The woman was … damn near impossible. *So why are you enjoying this so much?*

'Horizontal, it would mostly be moaning, and what words there were wouldn't make sense.' Cassie pointed to the nearest chair. 'Sit down!'

Jake found his frustration dissolving into laughter. She wanted him, no question, but she was fighting him every inch of the way. It was a new sensation and he was getting hooked on it.

And when she does surrender …

Cassie stifled a grin of triumph. She was ruffled and rumpled and trying desperately to hold on to her anger, but she was losing. Pure, feminine elation kept getting in the way. She'd felt how hard he was against her. For a second she blinked at a heady rush of power. To do *that* to a man … and a man like Jake. But fending him off, and controlling herself …

That's power, too.

He'd moved to the table and tugged out one of the chairs. He was holding it for her, politely waiting for her to sit. He was *sooo* cute when he did as she asked. When he didn't, he was something else entirely. *You like that too. In fact you like it—*

Cassie jerked herself out of that dangerous groove. Jake was still waiting for her to sit. She pulled herself together.

'Thank you.' She slid into the seat, and gasped as Jake sneaked a quick kiss to the side of her neck. Face completely bland, he stepped round the table to the other chair, dropping into it and folding his hands. If she couldn't still feel the burn of his lips on her skin, she'd have thought she imagined that lightning touch.

She put up her hand to rub the spot, then snatched it down again. *Forget it.* She shook her head, to clear it.

He was looking expectantly at her. 'Right then, Slick. Shoot.'

'Um.' It took her a second to regroup. She began to count off on her fingers. 'No one showed up from Villa Verdi, but four different people confirmed that two men and a woman stay there from time to time. One person thought they were brothers and sister. No one has seen them in daylight for a week or two, but there are lights and music at night.'

'That sounds sinister.'

'Why?' Too late, she saw the flicker in his eyes.

'Maybe they're all hanging upside down from a beam in the barn during the day.'

'Or sleeping in three coffins? Be serious!' she demanded. 'You know, we could simply go down there and knock on the door.'

Jake just stared at her.

'All right – I get it.' She held up her hands. 'I *do* remember what I said. We can't start straight in, interrogating them about Benson. But at least we could take a closer look. If

124

someone is there, we talk to them. We can always pretend to be looking for a lost cat, or something.'

'We explore other avenues first.' Jake was decisive. 'We need to concentrate on the restaurant in Menton. It's a much better lead.'

Cassie wanted to argue, but when Jake set his jaw like that, she knew she was wasting her time. She shrugged, pretending she didn't care that he was a bossy, overbearing ... male. 'Okay.' She gave in, despite the insistent urge to be *doing* something.

Jake gave her a narrow look. 'No slipping off to the Villa on your own. We do this together, or not at all.'

She dipped her head, not quite agreeing. 'What was all that stuff with Logo man? Mitch? He wanted to talk business?'

'Mmm.' Jake tipped his chair and balanced on the two back legs. Cassie bit her lip. He used to drive his mother crazy doing that. 'His approach was pretty crass, but the proposal might be worth following up.'

Cassie nodded absently. She wasn't much interested in Jake's money-making deals. She was still thinking of ways to get into the Villa Verdi. If she could come up with a really good plan ...

'How far were you involved with this Jason guy, the one who cheated you?'

'What?' Cassie's head bobbed up. 'What sort of question is that? There's no connection between Jason and Benson. And what the heck does it have to do with you, anyway?'

'Just answer. Were you sleeping with him?'

'I ...' Cassie squirmed a little. 'No, I wasn't. We

hadn't ... It wasn't like that ... We were building the business together ...' She sat up straight. 'There have *been* men, since you.' *Two, to be exact.*

'I wasn't asking about other men.'

'You walked out. You didn't even say a proper goodbye.' Out of nowhere, rage churned into Cassie's veins. 'You didn't answer my letters—'

'What letters?'

'I wrote to you.' *Every day.* 'I even tried to call you.' She saw something jump in his eyes. 'I had one postcard, one lousy postcard. *New York is great. Wish you were here.*' She still knew it by heart. 'And then, nothing.' Her voice choked.

'I never got any letters. I wrote to you. When I didn't hear back, I stopped.'

'I wrote them. I sent them.'

'They never arrived.' For a moment he looked at a loss ... uncertain. Cassie's heart twisted. 'I guess my dad ... I know he wanted a clean break. Said it was the best thing.' Jake shifted restlessly. 'There was so much happening. New York was amazing. Then there was Sydney, and Tokyo and Milan.' He wrenched a hand through his hair. 'I figured you were mad at me for leaving. That you'd thrown me over. And I did say goodbye. At least – I sent you a note.'

'I didn't get that either. But this is just old history.' Abruptly Cassie felt flat and tired, the excitement of the party draining away. She got to her feet. 'I think I'd like to lie down for a while.'

'Cool – I have some phone calls to make.' He let the chair legs drop back onto the terrace. 'Let me know what you decide about dinner. Or there's all that food in the fridge.'

Up in her room, Cassie slipped out of her dress and hung it on the wardrobe door, then pitched down on the bed. In a few seconds Jake had turned around everything she'd believed for the last twelve years. *He didn't write to you because he didn't receive any of your letters.* Her pulse kicked up with a jab of excitement, before realisation crashed in. *What difference does it make?*

He didn't love you the way you loved him.

She sat up, grimacing. He'd said the words, like all the boys did, as a way of getting into her pants. And as she'd wanted just as desperately to get into *his*, it was really no big deal. She'd made it more than it was. She'd wanted his heart, in exchange for her own. She shook her head. What a fool she'd been.

Well, the only way I want his heart now is barbecued, on a spit.

She still fancied him – most women would – but she was totally free of him. She hadn't lost his love. *Can't lose something you never had.* And all that was long ago, in the dim, distant past. She was in control here, which was just how she liked it. No one took power away from Cassie Travers. Whatever game Jake was playing now – probably relieving boredom until he got his mother's crazy bet out of the way – she was a match for him.

Suddenly hungry, she jumped off the bed and slithered back into the dress. The silky material was delicious against her skin.

Almost as good as Jake's mouth.

Chapter Nineteen

Jake stretched full length on the sofa, listening for the phone. He'd placed a few calls, now he was waiting for answers. He scrubbed the heels of his hands into his eyes. All that stuff with Cassie on the terrace ... It had all got *way* away from the information he'd been looking to extract, about this jerk Jason.

There was a strange chill in his gut. He'd left home at nineteen. What did a nineteen-year-old know? If he admitted the truth, he'd been relieved not to hear from Cassie. He'd loved her, sure he had – he shifted uneasily – but it had all been getting *much* too heavy and out of hand. He'd never suspected his old man of pocketing her letters, but it made sense. Sometimes post from his mother had gone astray too.

Things were dropping into place, with a very solid thudding noise. Bennie had warned him that Cassie hated his guts. He'd not really understood – assumed it was simply pique.

If she spent days – weeks – watching for the post that never came ...

Something twisted in his chest at the thought of the teenage Cassie, patiently waiting for the mail. He—

The phone rang. He hooked it up quickly.

'Yes?' He listened. 'That's good. We'll be there. Thanks – I owe you.' He slid smoothly to his feet. He had to lure Cassie into coming out to dinner. If she still wasn't in the mood, he'd have to persuade her. He looked at his watch.

Plenty of time. But it would be a bit of a bugger if she'd changed into jeans …

When he got to the stairs, Cassie was coming down. Still wearing the dress. His heart did a small but noticeable flip. She'd re-done her make-up and spritzed on fresh perfume. Jake inhaled the scent of lemons. 'Are you ready to eat? Do you want to try one of the other restaurants in San Remo?'

She looked down at him, head on one side. 'Sounds like a plan.'

Jake suppressed a grin as he reached for the jacket he'd dumped over the banister. *Perfect. No trouble at all.* 'And after dinner we can take a look at the casino.'

Cassie was eyeing him, with a speculative expression. 'Sudden urge to dispose of some of your money, McQuire? If you want, I can help you with that. So many shops, so little time.' She sighed heavily.

Jake shrugged into his coat, ignoring the provocation.

The casino building made an impressive show on the street, with white turrets and multi-coloured flags. Inside were sweeping staircases and tall rooms. Cassie stood back while Jake did what was necessary to get them admitted. *You could get used to this.* She wriggled her shoulders. *Dangerous thoughts.*

They stepped into a network of high-ceilinged rooms, lined with gleaming machines. Mechanical whirring and clunking and soft exclamations marked out winners and losers. Other rooms were set up for gaming on tables. Cassie recognised the roulette wheels, but the rest were a mystery to her. She spent a little time studying the players. Some were expensively dressed and glamorous, others completely nondescript. A grey-haired man in a shabby suit was gambling extraordinarily large sums on the spin of a wheel. A young couple in evening dress were whispering, heads together, deciding where to place their modest bets.

'Do you want something to drink?'

Cassie abandoned her people watching and focused on Jake. In a slouchy linen jacket he was worth focusing on. The hottest guy in the room and he's here with me. *Lucky guy.* 'Just mineral water, please.'

She drifted out onto a balcony while Jake found his way to the bar. The night was warm and the street below was brightly lit and buzzing with cars and people. She leaned against the parapet. Something was going on here. Jake was up to something.

'Are you going to tell me what this is about?' she asked, when Jake delivered her water. 'Why are we here?'

'I have a meeting.'

Cassie exhaled. 'A business deal! Why didn't I guess?' She considered him, eyes narrowed. His bland expression didn't tell her a thing. 'Well if you're going to be wheeling and dealing I'm getting myself a few chips, or whatever they're called, to have a flutter.'

'Here. Open your purse.' Jake reached into his pocket and folded a wad of Euro notes into the bag. 'You can use these to play the gaming machines.'

'Fine.' Cassie tossed her head. 'The little woman will go and amuse herself while you do whatever you do.' She'd all but spun on her heel, when Jake reached for her arm. 'Hold on a moment.' He tightened his grip as Cassie leaned away from him. 'This meeting involves you too.'

Surprised, Cassie shifted her thoughts away from the pressure of his fingers on her bare arm. 'Me?'

'Yes.' Sure he had her attention, Jake loosened his hold. 'That guy, Mitch, that we met this evening?'

'Logo man.'

'That would be him. He wanted to speak to me because he'd been approached to set up a meeting by a third party.'

Cassie frowned. 'And this matters to me because?'

'I think the man who wants to get to know me better is your friend, Jason.'

Cassie took a half step, swaying. The air shimmered a little at the edges. Jake's hand shifted to her waist, comfortingly solid.

'That's …'

'… an incredible coincidence. I know. But how many Jason Fairbrooks can there be in the world? Your instinct was right. He did head for the Riviera.'

Triumph put a shot of warmth through Cassie's veins. For about six seconds. Then the heat in her blood was pure rage. 'Just give me ten minutes alone with the rat.' Her fingers flexed. 'Then you can talk to what's left of him!'

'Spitfire.' Jake was looking at her with indulgent amusement that notched her anger up a peg or two. She stepped forward, until they were toe to toe.

'I can take you too, McQuire. Just name the time and place!'

'I live in hope of that very thing, but I never thought you'd ask.'

Jake rocked back gently on his heels. The intense flash in Cassie's eyes sent a flicker of excitement through him.

More than a flicker. Her scent made him want to inhale deeply and nuzzle her neck. This was neither the occasion, nor the place. *Unfortunately.*

Cassie was swearing inventively and fizzing with rage.

The temptation to stop her mouth in a very agreeable way was almost overwhelming. Jake conquered the impulse with a magnificent effort. For one thing, there wasn't time. He turned her slightly, rubbing his palm slowly down Cassie's spine, gentling her like he might an angry cat. And felt her relax.

After a few beats and some audibly deep breathing ... 'Okay. I'm cool.' She gestured with spread hands. 'I suppose you have a plan.'

'It doesn't involve physical violence – which I realise may make it less attractive to you.'

She blew out a breath, huffing her hair away from her face. Jake's fingers had been itching to brush that unruly strand from her cheek.

'I'm cool,' she insisted. 'Tell me.'

He studied her. She'd overcome the surge of anger. Her eyes were clear and assessing. Satisfied, he outlined his proposal. She considered for a moment. Jake held his tongue until she nodded. 'I like it. Simple, but it has class. I can't wait to see that worm's face. It's more civilised than kicking him in the ... knee.'

Jake smothered a grin. 'We're grown up now. Grown-ups do things differently.'

'Not everything.' The mad hadn't quite gone away. She was baiting him. It was working. The provocative tilt of her head had heat going where heat should not be. Not when there was a con artist to meet and greet.

Reluctantly he looked at his watch. What he really wanted to do… What he really wanted to do was totally unrelated to catching a fraudster. He bit off a sigh. 'I'll get back to you on that one.' *And that's a promise.* 'Curtain up in about five. You go that way.' He couldn't resist brushing his lips over her cheek as he gave her a little push. 'You know your cue.'

Cassie made her way to a small side room with more elaborate slot machines, the workings of which she didn't begin to understand. A careful choice of positions gave her a good view of Jake, in the gaming area. He was leaning against the wall, next to an unoccupied table. She shoved a few of Jake's notes into a machine, pressed some buttons at random and watched the other room.

Mitch had arrived and was threading his way towards Jake. A second man walked close beside him, head down. Her heart boomed in her ears. *Is it Jason?*

Cassie craned to get a better view. The machine behind her grumbled and pinged. She pushed the buttons again, to shut it up. The stranger stepped away from Mitch's side to greet Jake, giving her an uninterrupted sight of his profile.

Yes!

Cassie half rose from her stool to punch the air, remembered where she was and subsided, biting her lip. A woman sitting at a machine opposite was stealing sideways glances at her, frowning. Cassie bent to feed in more notes and set the machine whirring again. The inquisitive woman turned back to her own machine.

Jason was waving his hands, explaining something.

Cassie saw his fingers slide towards his mouth, a familiar gesture. He did that when he was nervous.

You'll be a lot more than nervous in a short while, my lad.

Anticipation coursed through Cassie, along with – nothing.

You don't feel a thing for him any more.

Her fingers flexed as she stared at the three men. Really, what *had* she seen in Jason? Compared to Jake, he was just a skinny boy with sloping shoulders, wearing a cheap suit.

Behind her the gaming machine gave a triumphant ping. She jumped, turned and gave a bark of laughter as lights flashed and the machine spat out a winners' slip. Not so much fun as a cascade of coins, but a lot more manageable. She was stowing it in her bag as Jake raised his hand in the signal. Heart thumping with excitement, she slid off her chair and glided into the next room, leaving her curious neighbour muttering in astonishment and envy.

'Darling, so glad you decided to join us.' Jake stepped forward, to draw her into the group. She grinned up at him as she heard the gasp from beside her. She counted to five, then turned.

'Hello, Jason.'

Chapter Twenty

Cassie had never seen anyone go so deathly pale and then so unbecomingly red, all in the space of a moment.

Mitch, confused, but astute enough to know something was going down, looked from one to the other, curiously. 'Hey, Jase, I didn't realise you knew Mrs McQuire.'

'Mrs ...' Jason was close to gobbling, Cassie noted gleefully. Like a turkey. He'd be trussed up and oven-ready if she had her way. *Down girl. Chill.*

'Mr Fairbrook and I are old ... business associates,' Cassie explained.

'Well, um, you'll to be able to speak for him then.' Cassie recognised the flash of alarm in Mitch's eyes as he picked up the tension swirling in the air. His gaze skittered wildly around the room. 'Er ... I think I see someone ... a friend ... just need to say hello. If you'll excuse me.' He backed away, fast.

None of them watched him go.

'*Mrs* McQuire?' Jason had got his tongue working, though his face was still scarlet. 'You're married to *him*?'

'You are not in a position to ask questions,' Jake cut in, low but deadly. 'Cassie would like a cheque for the money you stole from her, and an apology. Then you can go. You have your cheque book with you?'

'I ...' Jason's Adam's apple bobbed as he struggled for words. His hand went automatically to his jacket pocket, then stopped. 'I ...'

Jake looked bored. 'Just do it.'

Fascinated, breathless, Cassie watched as Jason produced his cheque book. She'd never seen or felt anything like this. Authority radiated off Jake like a force-field. He hadn't even raised his voice. Her stomach quivered.

Jason finished writing. His hand shook as he ripped the cheque from the book. He held it out to Jake. A curt nod had him thrusting it at Cassie.

Her hands were shaking almost as much as his when she took it.

For heaven's sake, Travers, get a grip. This is Jake – you've shared his sandwiches and drowned him in water fights and fallen asleep with him in front of the TV – though not lately.

She cleared her throat. 'Is the money still there, or will this bounce?'

'The money is there,' Jason croaked.

'I think Mr Fairbrook realises that there would be serious consequences if it wasn't.' Jake flicked Cassie a glance. 'Do you want to press charges?'

Cassie hesitated, chewing her lip. Justice and sweet revenge – but also police, courtrooms and dirty linen washed in public. She shook her head, and saw the most imperceptible nod of approval from Jake. Inexplicably her heart lifted.

Jake's attention was back on Jason. 'I've gathered quite a lot of information about you in the last few hours, Fairbrook. I'm sure there will be more to find. Enough to make your life very uncomfortable if anything should happen to the funds before that cheque is banked. You should be grateful that Cassie is generous enough not to want to see you in jail.'

Words were clearly fighting in Jason's chest, but they didn't come. He took a step back, turning away.

'Fairbrook.' Jake's voice grated. 'The apology.'

Jason flinched. He coughed, a hand to his mouth. 'I ... I'm sorry, Cassie.' The words were a barely audible mumble.

Jake crooked an eyebrow, checking if it was enough. Cassie nodded.

'Now, you can go.'

Jason hesitated for a second, then turned shakily to walk away. He was almost running by the time he reached the door.

'Phew!' Cassie let out a long breath. 'I think I may need a drink. A real one. With alcohol in it. You are seriously scary, d'you know that?'

'I have been told.'

'Remind me not to get on the wrong side of you.'

'Cass, you are probably the only person I know who *wouldn't* be afraid to take me on.'

They stood looking at each other for a long moment.

Cassie stared up into Jake's eyes and thought she detected a trace of surprise. He wasn't the only one. What he'd just said *might* have been a compliment, but she was too distracted to decipher it. Her knees were distinctly shaky. Everything had gone remarkably smoothly. Now it was over, she even felt slightly sorry for Jason. He'd come here, expecting to fix the deal of his life. And encountered ... one of the biggest predators on the planet.

She folded the cheque. 'Let's go home and have that drink,' she suggested. She extracted the ticket from her evening bag and held it up. 'After I collect your winnings.'

'I don't believe it.' Cassie paced back and forth along the terrace, nursing a small glass of brandy. Jake lay back in his chair and watched her. 'You mean to tell me that creep stole my money to try out a *gambling* system?'

'Yep.' Jake held up his glass and examined the whisky in it. 'He wanted me to back him. Your money was seed-corn – his share in a partnership. He was planning things on a big scale. He had it all mapped out – San Remo, Monte Carlo, then Atlantic City and Vegas.'

'He must be barking.'

'To think that the system would work? Or that I would be willing to risk putting money into it?'

'Both.' She thought of the cheque nestling in her handbag. 'I suppose I was lucky he hadn't already blown the lot.'

Jake was staring pensively into his glass and didn't answer.

Cassie stopped pacing. It was another soft, beautiful night, so how had the space between them suddenly got awkward and edgy?

'Jake?'

He looked up. The twilight was too deep for her to see his face clearly. He'd finished the last of the whisky. 'I suppose, now you have your cash, you'll be wanting to head back home?'

'No.' She was startled at the idea. Go back to Bath? Leave all this behind? Her stomach gave a strange lurch. 'We haven't figured out the Benson thing yet.'

'Ah, yes.' For a second he sounded hesitant. 'Benson. The search goes on.'

'Of course.' Cassie put down her glass, rubbing her hands up her arms. It was getting cold on the terrace. Or maybe it was a reaction to the exhilaration of confronting Jason? 'I think I'll go up. I can check for lights from Villa Verdi. You get a different view from upstairs,' she said brightly.

When she drew her bedroom curtains ten minutes later, the Villa below was in darkness.

Cassie lay on her back and contemplated the ceiling. She'd seen a whole new side to Jake tonight, and it had been ... exciting.

And let's face it, a little frightening.

And then he'd said that, about her being the only person to stand up to him.

As if! You'd just melt into a puddle.

Hmmm. She *did* know how to cope with Jake. Keep him at arm's length. If she let him kiss her, *then* she'd melt into a puddle. Which meant that she shouldn't let him kiss her. That way she stayed in control. That was right, wasn't it?

She rolled over and put out the light.

Jake stood on the landing and watched the light go out under Cassie's door. His head was scrambled. He didn't know what he was doing here. In Italy, in this house, standing on this spot.

On the wrong side of a closed door.

His mother had teased a promise out of him, then sailed off into the sunset before he could find out what it was that he'd promised. A spasm of regret squeezed his chest.

For some unaccountable reason an unsettling feeling was swirling around inside him – a feeling that time was passing, and he'd already wasted too much of it. *Weird, or what?*

He moved restlessly. Tonight had strung him out, wondering how Cass would be with this Jason guy. Whether the murderous talk hid the fact that she still cared for him. And then he'd realised that fixing for her to get her money back meant she was free. She could go home, right now, if she wanted.

That had been a stinger, right between the eyes, and he hadn't seen it coming. The relief he'd felt, when she said she'd stay ... The Benson thing had really hooked her. He leaned against the wall, frowning. The Benson thing. That was another can of worms.

Stepping forward, his hand hovered over the handle of Cassie's door. He could go in there, kiss her, make love to her. His muscles tightened at the thought – but that wasn't the way he'd decided to play this. He was holding himself to that.

Even if it does fry your brain.

Chapter Twenty-One

'And Jake made him give it back. All of it.' Cassie nestled the phone into her shoulder as she buttered a roll. She glanced up as Jake's shadow loomed beside her. He dropped into a chair. 'Benita,' she mouthed, stretching for the jam. Jake obligingly nudged it nearer. 'Oh, yes. The cheque will definitely be in the post. And then to the bank, please, at the speed of light.' She paused. 'I'll e-mail the Saunders report. Yes, until next week – sitting on the terrace in the sun, having breakfast.' She snorted. 'You know that envy is a very petty emotion – you too. Ciao.' She pressed the end-call button. 'This morning I have to work,' she announced as she put the phone down.

'I was about to say the same. I have to go out for an hour or so.'

'I'm missing you already,' she promised cheekily. 'Can you pass me a peach?'

Cassie dealt with all the business she could on Jake's sleek and shiny laptop. To her intense frustration, today the internet seemed to be down. Typing documents was fine, but that was it. No search engines, no e-mail.

Good-looking and infuriating. Just like its owner.

Glaring at the machine, issuing dire threats, shaking it, changing her position on the terrace – she even tried hanging precariously over the swimming pool in the hope of getting a signal – nothing worked. With a sigh she pressed save on her last document and closed the lid. Her morning's work would have to be faxed to Benita. If she could find a fax machine. And a printer.

She pouted, looking at her elderly, basic, bottom-of-the-range mobile phone, lying on the table. She could get a signal on that. Now maybe if she had an up-to-date, all-singing, all-dancing phone, like Jake's ... A top-of-the-range one, which was currently nestling in his back pocket, wherever he and his back pocket happened to be. With an effort she dragged her mind away from the picture of Jake's rear she'd inadvertently conjured up.

She relaxed in her chair, day-dreaming. Now that her money had been retrieved from Jason perhaps she *should* invest in one of those fancy phones – one that let you do all the stuff a computer could. Maybe she'd held out for too long against putting proceeds from the business into anything that wasn't one hundred and ten per cent essential? Good communications were essential. For next time she happened to find herself on the Riviera. Or maybe she could get one of those cute little tablets?

Hello? Who are you kidding? Even with last night's winnings, you owe Jake everything you're going to earn, for the next half century or so, for all those dresses hanging in the wardrobe upstairs. And don't even think about the shoes ...

With no more work to complete she changed into her most respectable set of underwear and swam for a while, then took a pair of scissors to her paint-stained jeans and created a serviceable pair of denim shorts, humming under her breath as she snipped.

She'd run out of things to do, it was still a good hour before lunch and there was no sign of Jake. She leaned on the balustrade of the terrace, her eyes drawn to the Villa Verdi. She couldn't remember whether the shutter of the window on the right had been closed when last she looked. It was open now.

She stretched, raising her hands above her head to work out the kinks. Exercise. She could take a stroll before lunch. Work up an appetite. *What's the harm in that?* And if her stroll just happened to take her past a neighbour's house?

Calling out to tell Vitoria that she was going for a walk, she crammed on her sun hat and set off.

The section of the road below the Villa Constanza was dusty and narrow. She flattened herself against a wall as a car speeded by. Thankfully it wasn't Jake. Extracting herself from the sweet smelling embrace of a lavender bush that was spilling down from above, she brushed a few narrow leaves off her shoulder. What if she did meet Jake? She was only taking a walk. She hadn't made any promises about walking. She hadn't made any promises at all. Jake was busy, and she was at a loose end. They'd come to the Riviera to track down Benson. If she found out something about the Villa Verdi Jake would be pleased and surprised. *And maybe just a tad impressed?* And she'd have shown him that she wasn't the clinging, needy type, who had to have a man to do everything for her.

So – that's all right then.

The gates of the Villa Verdi, when she reached them, were imposing and not quite closed. Taking this as an omen – practically an invitation – Cassie slipped through. She stood just inside, trying to get her bearings. The view from the Villa Constanza was deceptive, giving the impression that the house was closer to the road than it was. Ahead of her a driveway zigzagged upwards, through trees, with only a glimpse of the Villa Verdi above. If she wanted to see more, that was where she had to go. Straightening her shoulders, she began to climb.

'Cass?' Jake strolled through the lobby and the salon, and into the garden. The laptop, a bottle of sunscreen and what appeared to be two narrow tubes of paint-stained denim lay abandoned on one of the pool chairs.

'Signore?' Vitoria emerged from the side of the building, a broom in her hand. 'Ah – bella,' she exclaimed at the bouquet of freesias Jake was holding. 'For Signora? I put them in water.'

'Uh.' Reluctantly Jake handed them over. He'd been passing a kerbside stall and the bright colours and fragrant scent made him think of Cassie. He'd bought a large bunch on impulse. 'Where is the Signora?' Vitoria had buried her nose in the flowers, sighing appreciatively.

'Oh. She has gone out, for a walk?' Vitoria looked up, startled, as Jake cursed softly.

'How long has she been gone?'

'No more than venti minuti – twenty minutes? She said she was just going down the hill,' Vitoria explained, puzzled as Jake turned sharply on his heel, heading for the door. 'Signore? You go to search for her?'

'There's no need to search. I can guess exactly where she is.'

The climb was making her breathless. It had to be the heat.

It couldn't be far off noon and the sun was high overhead, in a deep blue sky. Hard to believe it was raining at home. She paused, taking off her sun hat to fan herself, shifting her feet uneasily. *Is this really such a good idea?*

What was she going to say, if there was anyone at home when she got to the house? A lost cat story really wouldn't do, and she couldn't pretend to be selling something. It would be a problem too if they didn't speak English. 'Buen duorno' and a big smile wouldn't get her very far.

Is this really going to help you find Benson? Or is it simply going to show your hand and mess things up? You don't have to go any further. It was a stupid impulse, but no one need know. All you have to do is turn around.

She was hesitating, torn between a small stubborn urge to press on, simply to catch a closer glimpse of the villa, or the sensible alternative of retracing her steps, when she heard the car behind her, approaching fast. She jumped quickly onto the grass beside the drive. *Looks like you're going to meet the neighbours after all.* Her heart was thumping against her ribs. *You're going to have to wing it – and hope they don't think you're crazy. Or maybe it would be just as well if they do?*

The car crunched to a stop and the driver swung out of it almost before it came to rest.

'Jake!' *Oh … sugar.*

'What the hell do you think you're doing?' He was advancing towards her, fury quite clear in his face.

She took an involuntary step back, before pulling herself together and standing her ground. 'What does it look like?'

'It looks like you're trying to make an enormous fool of yourself.' Hostile energy was coming off him like a flamethrower. 'What were you planning to do when you got up there?' He stabbed a finger in the direction of the house. 'Just snoop around? Or were you going straight up to the front door? What story have you cooked up? *Please* don't tell me it's the lost cat.'

Cassie's temper rose effortlessly, like a red mist. Guilt, the truth of the accusation and her own stupidity stoked the mist higher. She stuck out her chin. 'What if it is? At least I'm *doing* something.'

'Yes – something ridiculous. And it stops right here. You're coming back with me. Now.' He held out an imperious hand.

The spikes of guilt vanished in a puff of red smoke. She leaned forward, fists on hips. 'Where do you get off, McQuire, telling me what to do?'

'I'm not fighting with you on someone's driveway, Cassie.' He dropped his hand. His voice had fallen to an ominously low note. 'Get into the car. Now, please.' His eyes were doing a good impersonation of ice chips.

She got into the car.

The silence was at detonation point when they reached the Villa Constanza. Cassie spilled out of the passenger seat and hared round to Jake's side as he opened the door.

'Is this private enough for you?' she demanded as he uncoiled from behind the wheel. 'Because I want to tell you that no-one, *no-one* tells me what I can and can't do. Pin your ears back, Mister. You are one of the most arrogant, controlling—'

'Me? Controlling?' Jake spluttered. 'Cassie Travers, the one who always has to be in charge, in the lead, laying down the rules—'

'I'm *organised*.' Cassie's feet wanted to dance with fury. 'I like to get things *moving*. If you can't cope with that, then that's your problem. I'm not one of your air-head dates. I know what I'm doing—'

'Do you? Well I'm glad one of us does.' He put out an arm and yanked her to him. 'If we're talking about control, then try this.'

His mouth came down hard. For a second Cassie held herself rigid, then she simply melted against him, like wax.

In an instant the anger Jake was channelling into the kiss diffused and softened. He was teasing her mouth, not tormenting it – and losing himself in the process. *Oh, what the hell ...*

He gathered her in close, and gave himself up to the heat.

Cassie's head was ringing. *How can he* do *this?* Her brain was yelling *fight, kick, scream* – the crazy bit that didn't seem to understand that Jake's mouth and his body, and the perfect way they fitted to hers, well ... it was just too much bliss for one woman to resist. She kissed him back, with a fervour that had him clinching her so tight, breathing was almost a memory. When he finally let go, dropping his head to her shoulder, Cassie felt him trembling. Or was that her?

He groaned, straightening up. 'Remind me. What the hell am I trying to prove here?'

'That we're both out of control?' she suggested shakily.

He shook his head. 'Don't think that was it. Feels good though. Wanna do it again?'

For an answer, she wound her hands around his neck.

'I do *not* always have to be in charge.' She remembered her grievance when a basic and urgent need for air broke them apart.

'You do, so. You were always the one who told everyone what to do. You haven't changed.'

'You have.' For a wistful moment Cassie recalled the laid-back, easygoing boy she'd known. *That* Jake McQuire was as different from *this* Jake McQuire as the slim, rangy body she'd held then was from the hard, solid muscles that were wedged against her now. She traced a finger down Jake's shoulder. 'I suppose I do like to have things – as I want them.'

'Yes! We have an admission. Cassie Travers – control freak.'

'Takes one to know one,' she retaliated. 'What are we going to do, if we both have to be on top?'

'Sounds like it might be worth doing a little work on that one?' He grinned suggestively.

'Not on top *that* way.' She punched his arm. Actually the idea wasn't so unattractive. In fact … *Uh, oh.*

Jake peeled himself away from her, blowing out a breath. 'I'm used to running my own show, Cass – when I say, everyone jumps.'

Cassie stood up straight, squaring up to him. 'That goes for me too – at least …' She swallowed down a giggle. 'Well, there's only Benita, and she doesn't exactly jump. But it's the same principle. If it's there, go for it. I'd hate to be a clingy, needy woman.'

'No one could accuse you of being clingy.' Jake agreed, reaching to hook a strand of hair behind her ear. 'But maybe a little neediness is appealing? Now and then?'

'Pander to the male ego, you mean?' She shook her head. 'That's not me.' She shivered slightly. 'You take it or leave it, McQuire.'

'I don't think there's any doubt about that.' He gave her a twisted smile. 'I overreacted just now, at the Villa Verdi. That's a McQuire apology, by the way, just so you know.'

'I believe sorry is the conventional word.'

'Sorry it is then.'

'Jake, are you feeling okay?' She put up a hand, as if to touch his forehead. 'Don't answer that,' she amended hurriedly, when she saw the gleam in his eye.

'Huh. Now it's your turn.'

Cassie wavered, then bit the bullet. 'I apologise for getting impatient and sneaking off, *and* getting mad *and* calling you names.'

'Nicely done, Travers.' He looked at his watch. 'You want to go and try again to bother the people at the Villa Verdi, or shall we drive over to the French side of the border and explore Menton?'

An uneasy flush heated Cassie's neck. She had been … less than prepared when she went to the villa. And Jake had been so generous just now. 'Menton,' she chose. 'We can talk about how we approach Verdi on the way.'

'Whatever you say, ma'am.'

Cassie gave him a *look*, and got back in the car.

Chapter Twenty-Two

'This is heaven.' Cassie held her ice cream cone out to Jake. 'Want to try?'

He shook his head. 'I've got my own idea about what heaven tastes like.' He shot her a challenging glance that made her skin prickle. 'And it's not two scoops of pistachio ice cream.' He looked at her wonderingly. 'Where are you putting it all? We've only just had lunch.'

'A girl always has room for ice cream,' Cassie asserted indistinctly, as she demolished the last mouthfuls of her cone. 'Where are we going?' She peered doubtfully at the official looking building that Jake was piloting her towards. 'The Town Hall?' She caught sight of a notice as they walked through the entrance. 'Salle des Mariages. Marriage Room?'

Jake was handing over a palm full of coins to a lady behind a glass window who emerged, clanking keys, and ushered them along a corridor and through a set of double doors, then left them.

'Wow!' Cassie's eyes widened. 'This is amazing.' She turned slowly in a circle, taking in the full impact of the room. 'People get married here?'

Jake nodded. 'You can see the bans, or whatever they are in France, on the notice board outside.'

Cassie wandered around, fascinated. The walls and ceiling of the room were embellished with huge modern murals: angels and mythical characters and a fisherman and his sweetheart. The chairs were red velvet, the floor covered with leopard skin rugs. The whole effect was stunningly bizarre.

'I don't think the Registry Office in Bath looks like this. Who did it?'

'An artist called Jean Cocteau.'

'I've heard of him – but I thought he made films.'

'He did, plus painting and writing plays and novels. He lived here on the Riviera for a while. These murals are about sixty years old. Go on, say it. I'm a fund of useless information.'

'No.' Cassie tilted her head to study a fisherman whose eyes were painted in the shape of a fish. 'It's interesting.'

The arrival of another party was a signal to leave.

'Now where?' She blinked as they emerged into the sunshine.

'Just down here – I thought we might walk past a certain restaurant.'

'Where Benson may or may not have a meeting next Monday?' Cassie grinned. 'I like it.'

They strolled past. The restaurant was closed.

'Do you want to stop at the Villa Verdi on the way back?' Jake asked, as he settled behind the wheel of the car. They'd seen all that Menton had to offer, including a new building containing more of Cocteau's art, and the squat tower on the seafront that had been the first museum of his work. En route to the Villa Constanza they'd lingered for a while on the terrace of a tiny roadside café/bar, enjoying Salade Niçoise and excellent coffee, with an uninterrupted view of the sea. Now, in the bar's small, dusty car park, the evening sun was still hot, and the air sticky.

'Mmm.' Cassie pulled her door shut, doing up her seatbelt as Jake put the car in gear, and mentally deliberating between a shower or a dip in the pool once they reached home. The pool meant her improvised bikini.

'Was that a yes?'

Cassie dragged her thoughts reluctantly away from the effect of cool water on overheated skin. Villa Verdi was more important. 'Yes. And yes. But we still don't have a cover story.'

'Why not keep it simple?' Jake edged the car out into traffic on the main road. 'Sorry they couldn't come to the party, would they like to drop in for drinks?'

Cassie examined the idea. 'We're going to be getting a reputation as the most gregarious honeymoon couple on the Riviera.'

'Perhaps we've discovered we've made a hideous mistake, and can't bear to be alone in each other's company,' Jake suggested.

Cassie smiled but didn't reply. She'd already wondered, several times, what Vitoria was making of a honeymoon couple who slept in separate rooms.

'No one home.' Jake stepped back from the front door to squint up at the shuttered windows of the Villa Verdi.

'Can you hear something?' Cassie had her chin raised, listening. 'Running water?'

An investigation at the side of the building revealed an elderly gardener watering a bed of newly planted bushes.

'The owners are away for a couple of weeks,' Jake translated, after a short conversation.

'Oh.' Cassie couldn't keep the disappointment out of her voice. She shrugged. 'Well, we didn't need the cover story after all. Doesn't look like Gerald Benson is expected.'

'Benson.' The old gardener looked up with a smile. 'Si, Signora.' He delved in his pocket and held out his hand to Cassie.

Resting on the grimy palm was Gerald Benson's business card.

Chapter Twenty-Three

'He said the man had fair hair.' Cassie was pacing the terrace of the Villa Constanza, shooting questions at Jake as he leaned against the balustrade. 'It wasn't Benson. Benson was dark. You're *sure* he said blond hair?'

'As far as I could tell,' Jake nodded. 'Give me a break, Slick. My Italian isn't *that* good. The old boy had an accent you could stir with a spoon. Besides which, too much interest in what the mystery man looked like and the old guy would have wondered what was going on.'

'I suppose so.' Cassie twitched her shoulders irritably. 'If the man was fair, then it was someone else who delivered the card who was pretending to be Benson,' she reasoned. 'Tell me again.' Jake raised his eyebrows. 'Please.'

Jake gave her a long-suffering look. 'As far as I could make out, a fair-haired man in a red car called and left his card for the villa owner, with a message to ring him when he got back,' Jake recited obligingly. 'But as neither of us got a good enough look at the card to see the phone number, it doesn't get us very far, Cass.'

'Yes it does.' Cassie stopped pacing. 'We've got confirmation that Benson is involved in *something* here on the Riviera. We're going to find him, Jake. I'm sure of it.'

'Hey.' He leaned away from the balustrade to grab her by the shoulders. 'Don't get too wrapped up in this, Slick – it's a bit of fun, that's all.' He was frowning down at her.

'It's not fun if what Benson is doing is criminal.'

'If it is, it's not our job to take him down.'

'We might be the only ones who know that he's up to something.' She put her hands up to cover Jake's, where they gripped her shoulders. The intensity coming off him was throwing her off-balance. His face looked stern, almost hard, and yet she had a ridiculous impulse to stand on tiptoe to kiss the set lines of his mouth, to soften it out against hers, to pull his head down and bury her hands—

She swung away, out of his grip, to defuse a moment that had risen out of nowhere. 'So – I'm obsessed now, as well as controlling?' She forced her voice to sound jokey. How had they got themselves into this? And what was *this*?

'Don't put words into my mouth.' His voice was clipped, but the tension had drifted down a notch. 'I just don't want you to … to get hurt, that's all.' He'd shifted sideways, so she couldn't see his face. 'You take things to heart.'

'At least I have one.'

'And I don't?'

'Jury's still out. Have you ever been in love, McQuire?' *Now where did* that *question come from?*

'What's love?' He turned towards her again, his face still unsmiling.

'I think that would be a no,' she decided.

He was staring at her. 'Were *you* in love, with that Jason guy?'

'What?' Now he really did have her off-balance. 'I thought I might be able to be.'

'Why?'

'Because he was sweet and gentle, and I thought I could trust him.' Anger sparked, then died. 'Which shows what

I know.' *You thought you could mould him into someone you could love.*

Unlike the specimen in front of her.

Cassie surveyed Jake, suddenly feeling helpless. One hundred and ten per cent male, unpredictable, unmanageable. And smouldering at her now, like the air between them was going to catch on fire. She teetered on the brink. She could lean over and kiss him, or step back. With a sigh, she stepped. 'I'm going to get Benson, Jake. I can feel it in my bones. And I can take care of myself – but if I ever need protection, you'll be the one I'll call. Don't hold your breath though,' she warned as she made a creditable attempt at sauntering across the terrace, despite legs that seemed to be trembling. 'I think I'll go up.' She contrived an ostentatiously wide yawn, covering her mouth with her hand.

'Sleep well.' He'd retreated to the balustrade again.

She hesitated a moment, then turned and left.

Up in her room, Cassie picked up her briefcase from the floor and put it on the bed, but she didn't open it. Instead she dropped down beside it, scrubbing the heels of her hands into her eyes. *What have you got yourself into? What are you doing here?*

She'd walked into a fairy tale – the sunshine, the villa and its gardens, the beautiful room down the hall with the four-poster bed.

She shivered, although the evening was still warm. *It all comes back to Jake.*

A tremor of panic clutched at her throat. Even the clothes she had on, he'd bought. Somehow she'd let him edge up on her. His money was everywhere. Money – even getting back what Jason had stolen was down to him. He'd swanned back into her life, Mr Big-Shot, with his wads of cash and his fancy suits and his sexy smile – *no, don't go there* ...

With a groan she hunched up on the bed, hugging her knees. 'Cassie Travers, you are an idiot.' It wasn't just her surroundings. It was him. He was under her skin. *Back* under her skin, she corrected wryly. She fancied him rotten.

She shoved out with her foot impatiently, unbalancing the briefcase, which toppled onto the floor.

Was this how it was with your first lover? Was it something to do with memory? Did sex equal Jake, in her programming? She'd been *so* scared about doing it for the first time. Even with Jake. They'd done everything but – been almost-but-not-quite lovers for weeks. And then one evening, sitting on the sofa, at his house, watching a corny movie on TV, his arm around her ... He'd nuzzled her cheek, breathing the question in her ear. She'd turned her head. And there, at that moment, it had all seemed so right. She'd just let herself go.

And letting go had been the whole point, she discovered, with wonder – when everything that was feminine in her was overwhelmed by everything that was masculine in him. They'd melded together like two halves of the same coin. And she'd adored every second of it, helplessly in love.

Cassie felt a sudden rush of affection and half amused pity for the girl she'd been. Engulfed by the sparks that flew whenever she and Jake touched, she'd surrendered her whole self. A soft smile curved her mouth. Just like falling off a cliff. *How daft can you get?*

She'd never fallen like that since, and she wasn't going to do it ever again. Which left her with the sparks. Every time she looked at Jake, she wanted those sparks back. When he kissed her, her skin very nearly melted. She wasn't that silly little girl now, with romantic fluff in her head. What she felt for Jake had nothing to do with love and everything to do with good, old-fashioned lust.

But what are you going to do about it?

Jake cocked his head, listening. Was that the sound of Cassie's footsteps, overhead on the balcony? He concentrated, but he couldn't be sure. Idly he poured the last of a bottle of mineral water into a glass. Alone on the terrace, the temperature was dropping as shadows crept across the flagstones. He was hungry and there was work waiting for him. At the very least, he could check his e-mails. He dragged out his phone, then put it down. *Nothing going on at the moment that can't wait.*

The laptop was sitting on the chair where Cassie had left it. She'd recounted her frustrating morning as they wandered around Menton. He'd nodded in sympathy and promised to get her stuff to Benita. He glanced at his watch. No point in trying to send anything now. Benita would have left the office hours ago.

He looked up at the balcony. Maybe Cassie would come down again later, if she wanted something more to eat. *Or maybe you could just go and knock on her door?*

Abandoning the mineral water, he went in search of something stronger.

Chapter Twenty-Four

Cassie lay on her back and stared into the darkness. She'd taken a lengthy shower, read an article in a glossy magazine about buying a holiday home, and eaten half a melted chocolate bar from the bottom of her handbag, before settling into bed. Now her thoughts were chasing each other. Round and round.

She wasn't a complete fool. She knew when things were slipping out of her control – and Jake was definitely out of her control. She sat up, punching the pillow to make it more comfortable. But the problem wasn't in the pillows, it was in her head. *You were attracted to Jason because you thought you could mould him. Manipulate him into what you wanted.*

Stupid. And no basis for a relationship.

But is trying to revive the past any better?

Despite what she'd said about finding Benson, she really ought to be getting on a plane in the morning and flying home, to sanity and safety. To Bath and her work, where she really needed to be. She took a deep breath. She *would* fly home tomorrow.

Or …

Or she could stay here and take Jake as her lover again and see where it led her. Her insides went liquid at the thought, even when her chest constricted with alarm.

She sat up, pushing hair out of her eyes. *This is so crazy.*

She didn't know what Jake was up to. Why had he brought her here? She'd thought they were chasing

Benson, but now Jake's interest seemed to blow hot and cold. Sometimes it seemed as if he'd forgotten Benson all together. He could have any woman in the world, so what did he want with her? She knew what she wanted with *him* – oh boy, did she know. He'd made sure of that. He'd casually offered her his body and laughed when she turned him down. She took a second to admire his restraint, before recalling the knowing glitter in his eyes. Did that glitter mean that he was sure that eventually ...

She straightened up with a jerk. No way! She wouldn't give him that satisfaction. Rolling off the bed, she stalked over to the balcony windows, throwing back the shutters. It was a beautiful night. A full moon sent a silvery haze over the garden, the cool of the light in contrast to the perfumed warmth of the air. She leaned on the rail, chewing her lip. *Go? Or stay?*

Abruptly she made up her mind. She would go down to the garden, for one last look, but all this fake enchantment ended tonight. She could stay here for weeks and still not find out anything more about Benson. They didn't really *know* that he was involved in anything criminal. She would leave tomorrow. She'd return Benson's money, write Jake a polite note – thank you and goodbye – and talk to her accountant about making regular payments to clear everything she owed him. Then she would do her best to forget the whole dangerous interlude. And hope that nothing came back to bite her in the months ahead.

Tomorrow she would be on a plane back to England.

Jake slumped astride a kitchen chair, staring moodily at the tumbler of whisky in his hand. His discarded phone sat reproachfully beside an empty wine glass and a scatter of bread and cheese crumbs, from his late supper. As distractions, e-mails and food were failing miserably. *Which just leaves getting drunk?*

With a sigh, Jake put the untouched whisky down on the table and dropped his head, hands digging through his hair. Why had he gotten himself into this? He was just about holding on to his raging libido whenever he was around Cassie, but it was touch and go – and getting worse with every day that passed. When he'd first walked into her office it had been fine – well, not fine, exactly, but he'd been able to wing it. Now his skin burned every time she came within two feet of him. And *she* seemed to be able to enjoy his kisses and then bounce away, brushing him off as if he was a fly. Her head was full of chasing Benson.

Jake kicked back against the leg of the chair, wishing he'd never heard that name. How was he ever going to …?

None of this is going the way you thought it would. You are so completely screwed. And you only have yourself to blame.

Cassie wasn't like any other girl he'd dated, and he should have known it. He'd been so bloody confident. But like a fool, he'd fallen back on the usual stuff – the things most women expected – jewellery, clothes, trips to romantic locations. None of those influenced Cassie. What did you do with a woman who'd rather have an ice-cream and a clue to a bloody mystery? Hah!

He was up to his neck in the worst mess since … since …

There had never been a worse mess.

'If you could see me now, Ma, I guess you'd be laughing.'

He ground his teeth. Now he was talking to people who weren't there.

He shoved himself off the chair and began to prowl the dark kitchen. He'd been all set to sweep Cassie off her feet, and he was the one who was losing his footing. He wanted to kiss the living daylights out of her one minute, and shake her till her teeth rattled the next, and all she could think of was bloody Benson!

He uttered something between a groan and a growl as he came up against a wall, swivelled and set off in the other direction. Cassie wasn't impressed with his money, or his status. There were women in New York who would *kill* to be where Cassie Travers was right now. *Except they'd be in your bed, not sleeping in the room across the landing.* Frustration buzzed in his chest. He had to get stuck with the one woman in the world who was able to resist him. *And you picked her yourself!*

'Okay, hotshot, what's your next move?' He paused by the window, his eye caught by something pale, flitting amongst the roses. His mood lifted.

Looked like his next move was into the garden.

Cassie inhaled deeply, gazing round. The night had everything – warm breeze, the pale light of the moon, the scent of the roses and the jasmine. All it needed was a man.

'Couldn't you sleep?'

Jackpot!

Cassie turned slowly. Jake was still dressed, but the neck of his shirt was unbuttoned. She swallowed, remembering a chest lightly furred with dark hair. He squinted at her in the moonlight. 'That's a very fetching – thing – you have on.'

Cassie looked down at herself. The elderly T-shirt – short, shrunken, with a faded picture of Luke Skywalker on the front – was all she'd been able to find in her case suitable for night wear. What it had been doing in her luggage was a mystery.

'This? It's ancient.' *Soft and comfortable, but maybe not a girl's first choice for wearing in a seductively scented garden on the Riviera.* 'It's what's underneath that counts,' Cassie added nonchalantly, then winced. *Ouch! What on earth made you come out with* that?

'I'll take your word for it.' Jake smiled. A slow, melt-right-down-to-the-toes smile. Cassie's heart turned over. 'Unless—' He reached over her shoulder, to pick a perfect white rose and hand it to her. 'Come to bed with me?'

The exact same words as all those years ago.

Cassie looked down at the delicate petals of the rose, tipped on the edges with the palest of pinks. She raised her head to look into Jake's eyes. She took a deep, shaky breath. The garden swirled, and Jake's eyes flooded her with warmth.

Oh, what the hell—

'Why not?' She let the words out on a sigh, reaching to coil her arms about his neck.

They didn't make it as far as the bedroom.

Limbs impossibly entwined, they collapsed onto the sofa nearest to the French doors. Jake was kissing her throat, where the pulse thundered. The aged sofa gave a creak of protest.

'Jake, wait – I don't think this thing is up to our combined weight.' Jake's response was unintelligible, muffled against skin. Luke Skywalker went flying over their heads, followed by Jake's shirt. 'Jake!' She was laughing and breathless. It felt *so* good – but even so … She squirmed, grabbing a handful of dark hair to force his head up. 'This sofa is an antique.'

'Woman, will you stop going on about the bloody furniture! We'll buy them a whole showroom of antiques.' He stopped her protests, very effectively, with a kiss. In the wild confusion of mouth on mouth and skin deliciously on skin, Cassie forgot all about the sofa.

She wouldn't have noticed if all four of its legs had given out.

Chapter Twenty-Five

Cassie opened her eyes cautiously. She didn't want to find it had all been a dream.

It wasn't.

Jake was sprawled, face down, beside her. Out for the count. On the ceiling, painted clouds scudded across an azure blue sky. The warm pressure against her knee was Jake's leg, resting close to hers. The filmy drapes on the tall posts of the bed fluttered in the draught from the open windows. She let out a long, exultant sigh, attempting to piece together what she remembered of the night.

Heat, laughter, passion, in a heady blur of need and desire.

At some stage Jake had carried her up here, to the bridal suite. She recalled that much—

As to the rest ...

She stretched experimentally, her skin tingling. The chemistry was still there – all it had taken was for her to drop her guard. She gathered her lower lip into her teeth. Today she was supposed to be flying home. Instead here she was, lying beside Jake, having been comprehensively and extensively loved. And there wasn't an atom in her body that regretted it, she realised, slightly dizzy.

When Jake offered her the rose, with *that* look on his face. And whispered those *so* simple words ...

Suddenly it hadn't mattered that she'd vowed it was never going to happen.

They were having an affair. She could handle that. She

could handle anything. A grin turned up the corner of her mouth. She remembered doing several things in the night that had required quite a lot of handling.

She sat up slowly. She had no expectations, which was the important thing. Whatever this was, it was purely physical. She could walk away from it, any time she liked. *Any time.*

She lifted her chin. No clinging. No neediness. *Relax and enjoy.*

A small movement beside her made her turn. Jake was watching her sleepily. Her heart gave a strange, shifting lurch at the look in his eyes. They regarded each other for a long moment.

'Um,' Jake broke the silence. 'That was quite a night.'

'It was,' she agreed cautiously.

'I ...' He reached for her hand. 'Are you okay with this, Cass?'

'If you're going to tell me that the whole thing was a mistake—'

'No!' He sat up quickly. 'I just wanted to be sure ... You didn't have any regrets.'

'What's to regret?' She put a hand on his chest. 'I had a great time, you had a great time.' She tilted a provocative eyebrow at him. 'I'm guessing, here, but that was my impression. Although I'm not sure that antique sofa downstairs is ever going to be the same ...'

'Cassie Travers, you are incredible, you know that?' Jake reached for her and pulled her into his arms. Their eyes locked. She saw the glimmer of shock in Jake's, which must have been mirrored in her own.

'Just what a girl needs to hear, first thing in the morning.'

Her voice wobbled as she turned the moment jokey and saw his face flood with – relief?

Heart hammering, she squirmed out of his grasp. 'I don't know about you, but I'm desperate for a cup of coffee.'

'It doesn't mean anything. It doesn't mean *anything*.' Cassie powered up and down the pool, twenty minutes later. When a man and a woman spent the kind of night together that she and Jake had just spent, there were bound to be ... aftershocks. Jake had paid her a compliment and for a moment they both got a bit breathless. It was just low blood sugar. Caffeine depletion. Whatever. It didn't mean anything. That was a net she *couldn't* get caught in.

She turned on her back and floated in the middle of the pool. Independent, in control, nobody's plaything – that was how she was. Heart whole and fancy free, under the Italian sun. You could make a song out of it – one of those anthem type tracks, about free-spirited women, living their own lives. She drifted to the side and hauled herself out of the water.

Jake was reading the paper as she wrapped herself in a robe and towelled her hair. All she could really see of him was a pair of legs. How could a man's legs turn her stomach to mush?

'Bugger!' He put down the paper.

'What?' Cassie stopped her vigorous rubbing. 'Stock market gone down a point or two? Euro in crisis?' She scooped her half-dried hair out of her eyes and reached for the chocolate croissant Jake had cut up and put on her plate. Cramming a piece into her mouth, she sighed contentedly.

'Not that bad.' Jake watched, apparently fascinated, as she munched the croissant with relish, before snagging the other half. 'Some reporter has got hold of the marriage story.' He handed over the paper. 'Middle of the page.'

'Wow! Just what every woman dreams about, having her wedding announced in the financial news.' Cassie began to read, 'Jake McQuire, CEO of McQuire Projects, understood to be honeymooning in the vicinity of Monte Carlo, successfully disposed of his controlling share in ... blah, blah, blah.' She looked up. 'I'm crushed, McQuire. Here I am, meant to be the bride, and they didn't even mention my name.' Her grin died as she registered the frown between his eyes. 'It's not going to affect your business or anything, is it?'

He shook his head. 'It's just an irritation, that's all. Do you want another of those?' He indicated Cassie's empty plate.

She flopped into a chair, picking up tiny pieces of chocolate on the end of her finger and licking them off with enthusiasm. 'Are there any?'

'Maybe in the kitchen.' He reached for the basket. 'I'll go and find out, shall I?'

Cassie assessed the weight of the coffee pot. Finding it unsatisfactory she handed it over, with a blinding smile. 'This needs filling too.'

Jake looked down at it. 'Right, then.'

Leaning against the counter, waiting for the coffee to brew, Jake tried to put his raging thoughts in order. What the *hell* had been in his mind, when he said they could make use of the honeymoon mistake? He might have known the story would take on a life of its own.

But that wasn't the worst thing confronting him.

Memories were tumbling out around him, mixed in with flashes of the night they had just spent. Cassie at seventeen, beautiful and shy, the first time he kissed her breasts. Cassie four hours ago, kissing her way down his body ...

He put a shaky hand to his eyes. They'd just spent an amazing night together and Cassie was out there on the terrace, eating breakfast, *devouring* breakfast, as if nothing had happened.

He turned sharply, almost knocking over the perking coffee. What had he expected? Cassie wasn't that wide-eyed girl any more, hanging on his every word, admiring, adoring. She *certainly* wasn't one of his New York dates, casually angling for the bauble from Tiffany's, the hot new sports car, the trip home to meet her mother. Cass was ... Cass.

He snatched up the coffee pot, cursing as the hot liquid splashed on his fingers. He looked down at the reddened skin on his hand with a twisted smile. He'd offered himself to Cassie often enough, in an attempt to provoke her. He could hardly complain now if she'd enjoyed him the same way she'd just enjoyed that chocolate pastry. Recollections of Cassie licking chocolate off her fingers sent a quiver across his abdomen. Enjoyment was a two-way street. How difficult was it going to be, to entice her back to bed?'

'The pool men are here, Signore McQuire.' Jake looked up

from the laptop, glad of the excuse to stop scrolling down a long line of e-mails. All of them contained congratulations; most of them were fishing, with varying degrees of tact, for the name of the bride. One or two made assumptions that had Jake wincing. He was deleting those, fast. He didn't want to risk even a remote chance of Cassie stumbling on them.

Vitoria stood patiently beside the door, waiting to get his full attention. He punched a couple of buttons, casually slid the wireless card out of the machine and closed the lid, pocketing the card. 'Is there a problem with the pool?'

'They come ... to make sure that everything is working?'

'That's okay, tell them to go ahead. Is the Signora down yet?' He'd left Cassie in the bath. He'd come down only because she'd shooed him out. The floor had been an inch deep in lemon-scented suds.

He'd sat in front of the laptop for nearly five minutes, trying to remember how to turn it on.

'Si, Signore.' Vitoria dropped her eyes demurely, but with a small smirk quirking her mouth. Clearly she'd seen the state of the bathroom. 'In salon.'

Jake looked at his watch. If he went anywhere near the salon ... 'I have to go out, maybe an hour? Will you let her know, please? Oh – and that I've taken care of getting her work to her office?'

Sitting at the elegant rosewood bureau in the salon, Cassie hummed an old Beatles tune under her breath and punched the next number from her address book into her phone. She was bursting with energy and whizzing through her contacts. She'd already persuaded a famous academic to give a private lecture on Jane Austen to a group of romantic novelists, visiting from America, and sourced tickets to a sold-out concert, for a guy who was planning to propose to his girlfriend on the steps at the Albert Hall, when a shadow fell across the table. A male-shaped shadow.

'What did I just tell you?' She killed the call to her favourite hot air balloonists, stifling a giggle. 'I'm done with you until lunch-time. Go and play on the stock market, or something.'

Expecting no for an answer, she swung round, getting her mouth ready for a hello kiss, and stopped dead. 'Jason!'

Chapter Twenty-Six

'Left you on your own, has he, the new bridegroom?' Jason's voice slurred slightly. He looked really rough, she registered in a quick up-and-down glance: unshaven, with a crumpled suit and pallid skin. The red-rimmed eyes boring into her were glittering and angry. Cassie ran her tongue over her lip.

'Jake is around here somewhere, did you want—'

'Nah.' Jason cut her off, stumbling against a jardinière and almost toppling it, before he found his balance. He was drunk, Cassie realised, even as the smell of stale liquor hit her nostrils to confirm it. She stifled an impulse to shrink back in her seat. Jason was shaking his head. 'Don't want to see the boss man, want to see the boss *woman.*' He tittered at his own joke. 'Got to hand it to you, Cass, you're a fast worker. More moves than I gave you credit for. Got his ring on your finger, just like that.' He tried to click his fingers, and failed. 'Just ...' He seemed to lose the thread of what he was saying. Cassie got to her feet.

'I don't want to talk to you, Jason. I'd like you to go now.'

'Or what? You'll turn the big bad boss man on me?' He was shaking his head again, swinging it wide and grinning. 'He's gone, Cass. Out. Not here. It's you and me.' He took a step towards her. 'You and me. And we're going to do a deal. I reckon you owe me.'

'Owe you? You were the one who stole from me!'

'It was for *us*, Cass. My system ... Once I was winning ...' Vacant eyes drifted for a second, then he focused. 'You put *him* in my place. In *my* place.' He thumped his chest. 'Now you're going to pay me. I want fifty thousand, or I'll go to the papers, tell them all about the hot affair I had with the new bride. That's going to make the shareholders sit up and take notice, isn't it? Not going to make hubbie happy. Hubbie happy,' he repeated, wandering again.

Cassie's alarm was sliding effortlessly into irritation. 'You have absolutely nothing to tell, Jason Fairbrook. You and I never had an affair!'

'No – but I've got an imagination though.' Jason's eyes homed in abruptly, hard and beady. 'I can make stuff up. Lots of stuff. All the stuff you like. Dirty stuff. That's what they want.' He wiped his hand across his mouth. 'Press ... Internet ... *Someone* will pay me.'

Cassie gave a disgusted snort. 'I really doubt if anyone will be interested in your sordid lies.'

'Maybe ... maybe I won't do that then.' He stared vacantly around the room.

Cassie straightened her shoulders, bracing herself to hustle him out. 'I think—'

'No!' Jason's attention came back to her with a rapid about-face, his expression changing to tragic misery. 'I'll tell them what you did. Led me on ... that's it.' His expression brightened as he examined the new inspiration. 'I thought we had a future. I helped you with the business – put everything into it. All the ideas ... Yeah, that's it. You used me. Broken-hearted, that's what I am. You abandoned me, for a man with money. You give me my share, Cass, or I'll start talking.'

'That's enough.'

Cassie let out a squeak and turned her head. Jake was standing in the doorway leading to the hall. 'You utter one word to any reporter and my lawyers will start proceedings so fast your feet won't touch the ground.' Jake strode across the room, putting his hands on Cassie's shoulders and pulling her back against his chest, so that they faced Jason together. She breathed deeply, resisting the urge to lean heavily against him. 'You okay?' he asked in an undertone, close to her ear.

'Just hopping mad.'

'I figured that.' He lifted his head. 'My ... wife doesn't want talk to you any more, Fairbrook. You can leave the way you came in.' He nodded to the terrace door.

'Hey! Wait a minute—'

'Just go.'

'I want money.' Jason's voice rose in a whine. 'You've got to pay me. You've got plenty—'

'And none of it is going into your pocket. Get out.' Jake slid his hands from Cassie's shoulders and moved towards Jason.

Jason backed hurriedly away and onto the terrace, shambling dangerously down the shallow steps. Behind him the blue water of the pool shimmered invitingly. Jake followed him out into the sunlight. 'Go away and sober up, man, and stop making an even bigger fool of yourself.'

'Fool – who's the fool?' Jason suddenly began to shout. 'You sure it's not you, Mr Moneybags?' He took a clumsy step forward. 'How d'you know she's not a tart? Jumped into your bed fast enough, didn't she? Three months ago she was ready to marry me. I had her, just there.' He held up cupped fingers, waving them under Jake's nose. 'Just there. Palm of my hand – money, bed, business, I'd have had the lot off her—'

Cassie surged forward. 'Oh, you miserable creep—'

Jake put out a warning arm, stopping her path. 'He's not worth it, Slick.' He pushed Jason's outstretched hand out of his face. 'I'll tell you one last time – clear out, now, or I'll call the police.'

Jake was turning away, contempt in every line of his body. Cassie's eyes widened, darting from one man to the other, when Jason's right arm shot out to haul Jake back. She started forward – to do what, she didn't know – as Jason flailed wildly with a bunched left fist. There was a dull crunch as it connected with the side of Jake's mouth. Jake's answering punch caught Jason square on the chin. He flew backwards, staggering, almost steadying his backward lurch, but not quite making it, stepping back again, then again, in attempt to balance.

'Watch out!'

Cassie's yell of warning came too late. Jason had taken one step too far. For a second he tottered on the brink of the pool, arms wind-milling wildly. Then he fell over the edge, hitting the water with a resounding splash.

Nursing the corner of his mouth with the back of his hand, Jake picked up a towel from a chair and handed it to Cassie, to dry the splatters on her shorts. Jason's head bobbed up, water pouring off his shoulders. He was snorting and yelling, but staying afloat. Jake took the towel, dabbing his face as the two pool maintenance men came running, drawn by the noise. 'Excellent timing, guys.

You can take that garbage out of the pool and see it off the premises.'

'Ouch.' Jake flinched, then held still, braced against the back of the chair in the newly pristine bathroom, as Cassie cleaned his cut lip.

'Remind me ...' Cassie rinsed the cloth in the sink. 'Who was it who said that grown-ups do things differently?'

Jake made a face at her, gingerly flexing the fingers of his right hand. 'I have *never* punched anyone out like that before.'

'I have to say that as a starter, Jason gets my vote every time.'

'Yeah ... Well. He *was* drunk.'

'He began the rough stuff,' she pointed out, as Jake shifted restlessly. 'Hold your head up. This is nearly finished.' She patted on antiseptic. 'There you go, champ. It's the best I can do.'

Jake ran his tongue around the inside of his mouth, testing. 'That feels okay. Thanks.' She was still leaning over him. Close. He put his arms around her, pulling her into his lap. 'You could kiss it better.'

'It'll hurt. You're going to have a really impressive bruise.'

'I'll take my chance.'

'It's asking for trouble.'

'Just go for it.'

The look in his eyes weakened her knees and her resolve. She reached over and kissed the uninjured side of his mouth, very gently. Jake tightened his hold, drew her in, and did the job properly. 'You were right. It did hurt.' He grimaced lopsidedly. 'Worth it though.'

'There are words for people who enjoy pain.' She scrubbed at her own lip, making a face. 'Ugh! Antiseptic.'

Jake picked up a tissue and dabbed carefully at the graze.

'Want to try it now?'

'Hmm ... Yeah. I think I could risk it.'

She was frowning when they broke apart. 'All those things Jason said – can he make that sort of trouble?'

'No.' Jake shook his head emphatically. 'Because, as soon as he's sober, my lawyers will be speaking to him. Forget it, Cass. Forget him.'

She decided to overlook the dictatorial tone, given the circumstances. 'I'm sorry to have got you involved in all this. When I knew him in Bath, he seemed so different.'

'Bad judgement call. We all make them, Slick.'

'Even the great McQuire?'

'Especially the great McQuire.' There was a two beat silence. Jake's eyes were clouded.

'What?' Cassie put up her hand to touch his face.

'My mother. My dad abandoned her, then I abandoned her.' He shrugged, with uncharacteristic awkwardness. 'I did call her, sent postcards. She visited me in the States a time or two, but I never came back to Bath to see her. And I should have come back, years ago. It took her being ill ... It could so easily have been too late, Cass.'

'But it wasn't, she's recovering. And you did come back when she needed you. That's what counts.' Cassie held her hand against his cheek.

'You think?'

'Yes.' She let him go, and rose to clear the first-aid debris, aware that Jake's eyes were following her. She got a glimpse of his face in the mirror when she opened the bathroom cabinet. How the hell had she ever thought she wanted Jason? Jake was more of a man than—

She shut the cabinet with a click, stepping back as the basin emptied. Jake pulled her into his arms again.

'I was wondering ...'

'Yes?'

'Would you like to eat in tonight, for a change?'

'Mmm. And who's going to do the cooking?'

'Me.'

'You cook?'

'Uh huh.'

'This I have to see.'

'Doubter.' He reached to pull one of her curls. 'I'll have you know I went shopping this morning, before the entertainment at the pool. Prepare to be amazed. Now – do you want to take a drive along the Corniche this afternoon?'

Chapter Twenty-Seven

'This tastes—' Cassie paused, spoon to her lips, eyes dancing. '—delicious.'

'It's not done yet. The prawns go in last.' Jake took the spoon out of her hand and dropped it into the sink. 'How's the salad?'

'Under control.' Cassie picked up a sliver of the red pepper she was slicing, to nibble at it, offering Jake a piece. He accepted it, turning back to the sauce simmering on the hob. Cassie looked around the room and sighed. Except for the run-in with Jason this morning, she'd had a wonderful day, exploring the Riviera in the sunshine.

And now here they were, working in the kitchen together, as if it was the most natural thing in the world. She shifted slightly as Jake leaned across to top up her glass of wine. Trapping him with her arms, she reached for his mouth, backing him against the counter.

'Mmm – you interfere with the chef like that and this meal is going to get seriously delayed.' He was pulling her into him again when something on the stove began to boil over. 'Sod!'

Laughing, Cassie let him go. She took a sip from her glass. The wine was cold and fresh and slightly fizzy behind her nose. 'Where did you learn all this?'

'I took a class.'

'No kidding?' Cassie examined the idea, head tilted.

'I can learn things.' His eyes challenged her over the saucepans. 'When I do something, I like to do it properly.

This is just about ready.' He fished out a strand of spaghetti and tested it. 'Are we going to eat here, or in the dining room?'

'Here,' Cassie chose, lighting the candles.

Jake drained and served the spaghetti, topped off with sauce studded with prawns, and set the plates down on the table. 'Let's see if this works.'

Cassie tipped her head up questioningly. 'Works?'

'You didn't ask the title of the cookery class.'

'But you're going to tell me.'

He grinned. 'Food, Wine ... Seduction.'

She dug her fork into the pasta. 'I'll let you know.'

Cassie loaded the dishwasher. It was the least she could do. Jake had served a dessert that involved eggs and sweet wine that had danced on her tongue. It had left her feeling exceptionally mellow. Now he was brewing coffee. 'What's that tune you keep humming?'

'Was I humming?' Cassie puffed out her lower lip. 'I—' The ringing phone cut her off. Jake flipped it off the wall. 'Caio?'

Cassie slotted in the last of the dishes and closed the dishwasher door. Jake muffled the receiver against his shoulder. 'Drinks, lunchtime tomorrow, next door?' He tilted his head to indicate up hill. Not towards the Villa Verdi. *Even so, there might be some information.* Cassie nodded enthusiastically. Jake grinned and went back to the phone, slipping into Italian. Cassie picked up the tray loaded with the coffee pot and cups and wandered through to the salon, smiling as she checked out the health of the antique sofa. It was hanging in there. She had curled up in a more comfortable seat, and was sipping her coffee, when Jake reappeared. 'We're invited for noon tomorrow. We don't have to stay long.'

'No, it's cool. Maybe we'll pick up some useful local gossip.' She set down her cup carefully. A pleasant day and a good dinner didn't mean losing sight of the ultimate objective. They still had to locate Benson.

Jake was sorting through the CDs in a rack above the expensive sound system. 'Where did you learn Italian? Was that a class too?' Idly she ran her finger round the rim of her empty cup. The quality of the silence made her look up. Jake was fitting a disc into the player. It seemed to be taking a high level of concentration. *Maybe* he hadn't heard the question ...

Cassie laughed. 'Pillow talk! Who was she? I'm sure she was beautiful.'

A Chopin Nocturne floated gently into the room. Jake leaned against the wall, watching her narrowly. 'Where are we going with this, Cass?'

'Nowhere. I'm curious. You know that.'

'Hmm.' He looked doubtful, then capitulated. 'All right, yes, she was beautiful. Her name was Chiara. She was the daughter of one of my father's business associates. We dated for two years. He wanted me to propose.'

'But you didn't?'

'She ran off with the mechanic who serviced her car, before I got around to it.'

Cassie flopped against the back of the sofa, laughing.

'Hey,' Jake protested, voice flat. 'The male ego is a fragile thing, Travers. You should be careful about laughing at a man when you're sharing his bed.'

With a stab of concern at the change in Jake's voice, Cassie sat up – to find him grinning at her. 'You ...!' She threw a cushion at him.

He fielded it easily 'Gotcha!' Cassie stuck out her tongue. 'Is that the recompense I get for all that cooking?' Jake turned his back to stash the cushion on the antique chaise.

Cassie tilted her head, studying an excellent rear view. 'I'm thinking of an appropriate thank you.'

'Sounds promising,' he approved, as she patted the sofa beside her.

'It will be.' She smouldered from under her lashes. 'If I'm not too full to move.' She leaned forward to top up their coffee cups, as he settled beside her. 'So ... given your usual choice of companions, what are you doing here, with me?'

Cassie put down the coffee pot to look over her shoulder, surprised at Jake's abrupt stillness. His face was curiously blank. Then he stretched elaborately, rolling his shoulders before dropping his arms. 'Cass, if you don't know why, then there is something seriously wrong with your memory.' He slid his arm along the back of the sofa, to hook her closer.

'You can remind me – in a minute ...' She fended him off with a well-placed elbow. Suddenly it seemed important she should know. 'Why me?'

'What do you mean?' Frowning, Jake gave up his attempts to pull her into his arms.

'I'm not beautiful, or talented, and I certainly don't have money or connections. So, what am I doing here?'

Jake shrugged. 'Because you want to be here? Because I want you to be here?'

'Not good enough.'

Jake sat back, still frowning. He was watching her narrowly. 'You're not going to let this go, are you?'

Cassie shook her head.

Out of nowhere, her heart was suddenly beating way too fast.

Chapter Twenty-Eight

He'd panicked, just for a second, but there was no suspicion in her face. Just Cassie, asking questions as usual. Half way between irritation and something else – something he didn't much like the feel of – Jake ground his teeth. He could see from the rapid rise and fall of her chest that Cassie's breathing had speeded up, and probably her heart beat too. But not in the way he'd planned for this evening.

He'd identified that other feeling now ... disillusion. When it came down to it, Cassie was just like every other woman – fishing for compliments. *That's* what she was getting at, not any other reason.

Only one way to finish this and move on. Tell her what she wants to hear.

He gave in. 'All right. You're lovely, intelligent, nice body, *great* legs, you have a crazy sense of humour – you want me to go on?' Expecting a wisecracking response, Jake felt his stomach clutch as he saw tears shining on Cassie's face. He grabbed her shoulders. 'Slick ... what the hell?'

'You really think ... all those things?'

'Why else would I have said them?' He pulled her into his chest, irritation dissolving – to be replaced by alarm as a sob shook her.

'I'm sorry,' Cassie hiccupped. 'I'm making your shirt wet.'

'To hell with the shirt! Cass, talk to me. What's the

184

matter?' He held her close as she tried to pull away. *What the hell?*

'I think I've had a little too much to drink.' She wiped moisture off her face with the back of her hand. 'I *never* cry.'

'I know you don't.' Jake gathered Cassie into his lap and held her. 'So ... what brought this on? Besides the wine?'

'Sensory overload?' She gave a watery laugh that wobbled in the middle. 'You, being nice to me? I'm not used to it.'

'I might have known it would get around to being my fault.' He was relieved to hear the familiar Cassie note coming back into her voice. 'And I'm always nice to you.'

'In between telling me what to do!'

'That too.'

Cassie pulled herself upright, moving a little away from him. The sudden, frightening gap that had appeared in her chest, leaving her fighting with tears, seemed to be closing.

'I ...' She hitched up a creaky laugh. 'You know what I'm like, I'm used to being tough Cassie Travers, always on the case. Tonight – maybe not so tough. Can't hold my liquor.'

Jake lifted his hand to brush her hair away from her face. 'It's more than that though isn't it? No, don't turn away from me. You can cope with anything, so why would you back down over the truth? Cass, I've told you before, any man would be proud to have you on his arm *and* in his bed. And if he's not ... Send him round to me. I just discovered that I have an excellent right hook.'

Cassie dropped her head, so that their foreheads

touched. 'You're nuts, you know that? Plus you have a new and disturbing interest in violence as a problem solver.'

'The next class will be anger management,' he promised, shrugging her higher on his knees, so that he could see her face. 'Something just happened here. A little bit of Cassie Travers that doesn't get much daylight came bubbling up. I want to know why.'

Cornered and imprisoned by the warmth of his arms, Cassie clenched her fists. *Oh hell ... He isn't about to let this rest ...*

She shut her eyes, swallowing hard. 'Things ... like you just said. I don't believe them. Can't believe them. They're not me. I don't have all that charm and beauty stuff. That's why I have to keep control of my life – work hard, be organised. *That's* what makes me a person.'

'Cass!' His hands gripped her. 'Hell – someone did a real number on you. Who was it – that Jason guy?'

'No.' Cassie opened her eyes, keeping her head down. 'It was before then. But it's old news. I don't want to talk about it.'

'Cassie.' His tone held a world of warning.

She ran her finger along the sleeve of his shirt. Smooth, expensive cotton. Even something that simple proved how far apart they really were. *Honey, do you need proof?*

'Cassie.' Jake's voice had dropped, warm and persuasive. A shiver went down her spine.

'You remember my mum and dad?'

'Vaguely.'

'Yes. So do I. Vaguely.' She heard the bitterness seeping into her voice. Bitterness she'd controlled ... forever. Tonight she couldn't seem to keep a lid on her feelings.

Jake was drawing something out of her. *Like a snake charmer.* 'I didn't know it then, but I can see it now. They were one of those couples who were everything to each other. I was just an encumbrance – physical proof that they loved each other, but otherwise an inconvenience. I spent my whole childhood trying to get their attention. Nothing I did was ever quite enough.' She paused, staring painfully into the past. 'I wasn't as beautiful as my mother. Or as talented. Could never be. My dad told me that. I won a little silver cup once, at the school sports day. I was so proud. I thought ... at last ...When I brought it home, he laughed at it, took me into the sitting room – it was their room. I was never allowed in there. He showed me the trophies my mother had won. There was a whole wall of them. When she was young she was a champion skier. I didn't even know. My mother ... My mother was always telling me to be independent. Stand on my own two feet. Around them I felt awkward, in the way ... Then I got older and something else—' She shook her head fiercely. 'It doesn't matter about that. I was good in school, I worked hard. I had friends. It didn't matter if my parents were ... distant. And I found that if I could control things outside, I could control things inside. And that was a skill worth having. And people were willing to pay me to make problems in their lives disappear. So I did. Pretty stupid story really.'

'Not stupid at all.' Jake ran his hands down her back, soothing, softening the tension that had crept into her muscles. 'I always thought it was cool, the way your parents just let you get on with your life. Especially when Ma was in my face about something. I didn't realise ...'

Cassie shivered. 'Why would you?' She tried a lop-sided smile. 'Now you know why I'm a control freak. What's your excuse?'

'Natural aptitude.' He raised her chin with his hand. 'Your parents were wrong, Cass. So wrong. They should have been so proud of you.' His eyes trapped hers, holding them. She wanted to believe him. Somewhere under her ribs, warmth began to steal through her. She doused it, before it could take too much hold.

'Thanks for listening.' She scrambled off his lap. He let her go. 'I think I'll go upstairs and wash my face.'

Jake ran his fingers down her arm. 'You do that. I'll lock up down here.'

In the bathroom Cassie took a long look at herself in the mirror. She wanted to believe Jake when he told her she was lovely. She had believed him ... once. It hadn't only been her parents who had made her what she was. They'd only started the process. There'd been a boy. A boy who had made her come alive. A boy she'd given her whole heart to. A boy who'd left and never looked back.

'It was you, Jake,' she whispered as she put out the light. 'You were the one who did the number.'

She started as she found him waiting for her on the landing. He kissed her then, tenderly, drawing her into the bedroom, to make love to her with a gentleness that almost stopped her heart.

And then he held her, until she fell asleep.

Chapter Twenty-Nine

Jake leaned against the car and pretended to study the travel guide he'd just taken from the glove compartment. His mind was scrambled. Cassie's revelations of the night before had touched him to the core. His respect for her had rocketed off the scale. Respect – he'd never thought of that word in connection with his little Slick before, but it had always been there, he realised, with a jolt.

What she'd said about her parents, it explained a lot about who Cassie Travers was. And made his own position a whole lot worse. Some time, soon, in the next twenty-four hours for sure, he was going to have to find a way to tell her what was really going on in San Remo. And – God help him – why he'd chosen her.

He braced himself against the car. There was such a thing as being too clever. And he'd been just that. In spades.

What the hell did you think you were doing, McQuire?

Actually, he knew the answer. Back then, when he'd made the plan, Cassie had been ... She'd just been a means to an end. But now ... He had to make it right with her. If he had to eat crow, and he guessed that he would, then he was going to have to get used to the taste.

Up in the bathroom, Cassie's hand shook slightly and she nearly jabbed her mascara brush into her eye. 'Dammit!' She winced and wiped a spidery black trail off her cheek. She rammed the wand back into its cylinder with more force than was necessary. She was so mad at herself she could *spit*. Where had all that stuff come from last night? She'd thought – no, *knew* – that she was over all that about her parents, a long time ago. Since they'd retired to live in Spain, she rarely saw them. She didn't think of them, didn't talk about them, certainly didn't hark back to her childhood insecurities. But last night she just hadn't been able to stop herself. What the hell must Jake think of her? That she was pre-menstrual or just plain crazy?

She crunched down hard on the memory of his arms around her, the sense of relief as it all spilled out, the touch of his mouth, and that long lean body, as they exchanged love in the darkness. She'd made a complete fool of herself, with all that needy stuff. Exactly the thing she always feared most. The thought made her feel slightly sick. Now Jake was looking at her as if she had ten seconds to detonation. And every time she met his eyes she felt a hollow in her chest like a shell hole. Somehow she had to get things back to what passed for normal in the Villa Constanza.

Behind her, perched on the edge of the bath, her mobile phone warbled, then fell in with a crash. Cassie fished it out, blessing the fact that the bath was empty. She pushed buttons to bring up the text message.

'Eureka!' She almost kissed the phone. This was just the thing. She shoved open the bathroom window and dangled out. Jake was below, standing beside the car. For a second she lost her breath. He was so damn gloriously, achingly sexy in very dark shades and white shirt. Sensation hit her in every nerve point. And some extra ones she'd only discovered in the last two nights. He looked up, locating the sound of the window opening above him. And, dammit, the damage to his mouth, inflicted by Jason and still faintly visible, only added to the dangerous appeal. He looked like a marauding pirate. One who could take care of himself, and his woman, in a fight. She shivered.

'Hey, McQuire!' Gulping in a breath, Cassie waved. 'Want to come on a treasure hunt?'

The stalls snaked along the main street of the tiny village. Folding tables, the boots of cars, blankets on the ground and some posher set ups that were obviously professional. The pocket-sized village square had long trestles, divided into pitches. All were full of wares for sale. Old books and maps, linen, vintage clothing, shoes and hats, ornaments, lamps, watches and jewellery, mirrors, china and porcelain. An open sided van parked at the end of the square was doing a brisk trade in coffee and pastries. Locals in their Sunday best mixed with tourists in shorts and T-shirts. Children and dogs chased each other in and out of table legs.

'Brocante.' Jake took Cassie's arm as they hit the first of the stalls.

'Or whatever the Italian equivalent is,' Cassie agreed. 'I have a standing commission from some of the shops in Bath to look for quirky stuff to dress their windows.'

'*Quirky stuff.*' Jake covered his eyes with his hand for a second. 'Don't tell me,' he continued ominously. 'I have a deep foreboding already. My role in this is to haggle, *in Italian*, for whatever disreputable piece of junk you've got your sights on.'

'Well …' Cassie grinned at his tortured expression, then relented. 'You don't need to look like that. Most of the stall holders will have some English – or American. A couple of the professional traders come to Bath on a regular basis. That's how I know about it. It all looks a bit haphazard, and the place is barely a dot on the map most of the time, but it has a good reputation. I'd forgotten about it. Benita sent me a text this morning, reminding me.'

'Remind *me* to thank Benita.'

Cassie dug her elbow into his ribs. 'Don't be such a spoil-sport. It's treasure hunting. It's fun. We're bound to find something good. Something different. This trip to Italy has turned out to be very worthwhile. And to think I didn't want to come.'

'We try to please. Good grief!' Jake was staring in fascination at a large and ornate piece of silverware, prominently displayed on one of the stalls. 'What is that? Apart from hideous?'

'An epergne?' Cassie suggested, putting her hand to her mouth to cover her giggles. 'Come on.' She grabbed his hand. 'I think the furniture is down this way.'

'Furniture,' Jake echoed hollowly. 'You want to transport *furniture* back to Bath?'

'Only if we find something *really* good.'

Cassie sipped her glass of Prosecco, taking in her surroundings with an appreciative glance. The garden here, the next-door neighbour to Villa Constanza, was completely different, very traditional with formal beds and statues amidst gravel paths, and even a fountain with marble seahorses. She wandered closer, for a better look, careful to keep away from the spray of water which bubbled and frothed, as she trailed her fingers in the fountain's basin.

She'd had an excellent morning. She'd bagged a wire birdcage – after a good scrub it would be gracing the window of one of Bath's classiest dress shops – plus a carved musical box for one of the jewellers and three vintage posters, advertising the charms of the Riviera, in deliciously faded pastels. They would probably appeal to the owner of a new bookshop. She'd baited Jake for a whole five minutes, feigning interest in an enormous chest of drawers, before he'd rumbled her. He'd led her away, with a firm hand under her elbow, and silenced her protests by kissing her – which had been her plan all along. Getting into the swing himself he'd haggled, in rapid Italian, for a handsome pair of silver candle sticks, emerging breathless and triumphant.

As Cassie had hoped, a couple of hours rummaging amongst the heaps of mingled treasure and junk had eased any constraint between them. But she had to be on her guard now ...

'You're staying to lunch, of course?' Cassie started as her hostess slipped an arm through hers. 'My son and daughter-in-law are so looking forward to meeting you.' Cassie blinked, stifling a grin. An awful lot more people wanted to meet Mrs J. McQuire than they did Ms Cassie Travers. A sudden stab of guilt assailed her. What had started out as a small white lie seemed to be growing bigger and bigger. Jake would have to ... She jumped back from her tangled thoughts when she realised her hostess was waiting for a response.

'It's very kind of you to invite us,' Cassie murmured. 'I need to check with Jake.'

'Of course. I wonder where—' The woman looked round. 'Ah! Over there.'

Jake was standing on the other side of the fountain. In conversation with a young woman. She had her hand on his arm. She was tall, blonde and beautiful, Cassie observed hollowly. As she watched, Jake detached the perfectly manicured hand from his arm and began to move away. Cassie clenched her fingers in the folds of her skirt. Her nails were short, serviceable and un-polished.

'Here's your gorgeous husband now, coming to find you,' their hostess announced with satisfaction. Cassie barely heard her. Jake's eyes had picked them out from the crowd. He was walking straight towards her. The sound of the falling water, of chattering voices, of the music playing softly, somewhere inside the house, faded away. Cassie was only dimly aware of the woman by her side and the blonde, left alone by the fountain.

Jake smiled that slow, killer smile and something in Cassie's chest lifted and blossomed.

Oh bugger, I'm falling in love with Jake.

Again.

Chapter Thirty

Cassie tried to concentrate on the delicious food she was putting into her mouth, and on the conversation going on around her. It was hard. Panic and joy were chasing each other around her system in waves. As the zing of love got the upper hand she wanted to jump up on the table and sing. Then reality crashed her back down again. What was there ahead of her but pain? Familiar pain. In the dark of the bedroom and the heat of passion Jake whispered many things to her, but love wasn't one of them.

Jake doesn't know what love is.

And she'd carelessly let herself tumble headlong ...

She almost groaned aloud, catching herself in time and reaching for her water glass. Across the table, Jake caught her eye and winked. She felt the soft brush of his foot against her calf and everything in her dissolved. This whole thing was a fantasy, a golden dream that had to have an end.

In that single second she knew, with complete conviction, that she'd rather have had the dream than not. She was living a fairy tale that many women could only imagine. And it was worth it, even if her nights ever after would be cold and bitter. *You can't undo love.* Every moment, from here on, must be etched in her memory. *The place, the time, the man.* Memory she could fall back into, during those long, cold nights.

Jake lounged back in his chair on the other side of the table, watching Cassie peel and quarter a peach and pop a slice into her mouth. A tiny trickle of juice on her chin was begging him to lick it off. He shifted restlessly in his seat. He'd like to be somewhere private, very private, feeding her that peach, a sliver at a time. Tasting juice and warm skin, sliding his hands ...

He sat up with a jerk, pulling himself back to his surroundings. He allowed the erotic image to fade, with reluctance. A glossy brunette with a man-made cleavage, sitting on his right, was in the middle of a vapid piece of gossip and casting subtly sidelong glances at him, under her lashes. He schooled his face to a polite mask and his mind to tune her out, concentrating on Cassie. Mercifully, she'd finished eating the peach. Watching her drink coffee was a lot less ... stimulating.

The woman beside him was still talking. He stifled a yawn. Cassie would have known in a minute that he wasn't paying attention to what she was saying. He'd probably have got an elbow in his ribs, to remind him to listen. Not that he needed reminding often. What Cassie had to say was usually worth listening to and if you *did* want her to be quiet – well, there were very enjoyable methods of doing that too.

His eyes lingered on her face. Studying her, he couldn't decide whether her mouth or her eyes were her most appealing feature. The expressive eyes were glinting green today, reflecting the halter top she had on. Her mouth was ... well ... soft, luscious, inviting.

He frowned slightly. She was looking a little pale. He'd noticed it when he found her by the fountain, after he'd shaken off the blonde with the red talons. *She'd* been stalking him around the garden, trying to get him to meet with her boyfriend over some business proposal. It had been a relief to see Cassie arm in arm with their hostess. She'd had a strange, startled look on her face as he'd claimed her.

There was still a trace of it now, in the shadows under her eyes. *The aftermath of last night?* He wasn't fooled. He'd known the trip this morning had been as much about getting back to their old footing as chasing props for dressing windows. Cassie had done successful business and had relaxed as she did it, growing comfortable in his company again. *Memo to self – Buy Bennie a dozen red roses for sending that text.*

Jake's jaw tightened as he remembered Cassie's tears. Her parents had been grade-A jerks and he'd never realised. At seventeen she'd been cool, clever and independent. She'd intrigued him. He'd been so hot to get into her pants, he'd never thought about how she'd got to be so self-contained. But now he knew. And he knew how it felt to have her soft and vulnerable in his arms. That felt better than it should. He didn't want Cassie hurting, but he couldn't deny the caveman rush over comforting her. What the hell, she'd never know.

You'd better make damn sure she never does, or your skin won't be worth a cent.

Across the table he met Cassie's eye and grinned, watching her face light up. He put his palms down on the table and prepared to push back his chair. They'd been sociable, now it was time to say thanks and go. He wanted Cassie to himself again. Without distractions.

'Is it always like this around you, McQuire?' Cassie

strapped herself into the passenger seat of the car, waving to their host and hostess who were standing on the steps of the villa.

'Like what?'

'Everyone you meet wanting to make their number with you?'

'Pretty much.' Jake was concentrating on navigating through a pair of narrow gates. 'It's not something I'm going to miss.'

'Miss?' Cassie slewed round to look at him.

'By the end of the year I will have shed all my current commitments, except Kings.' He checked the road for oncoming traffic. 'I told you I could be back in Bath for good.'

'I didn't know—I didn't realise you were giving everything else up.'

'Yep.' He shot her a glance. 'That's classified by the way. Only you and five other people in the world know it. I'm probably supposed to kill you now that I've told you.'

'My lips are sealed.'

'I hope not.' He cast her a brief, wicked look, reaching out to brush her hair away from her face. 'Tired?'

'No.' She was still taking in the idea that Jake wasn't going back to New York. Ever.

'I thought you looked pale, when we were having lunch.'

'Trick of the light.'

They'd reached the entrance to the Villa Constanza. Jake braked, with a questioning look. 'In or on?'

'On,' she decided without hesitation, pointing down the road, away from the villa. 'What's in that direction that we haven't already explored?'

'Dolceacqua? The artist Monet did a painting of a bridge there.'

'Then let's go and see what Monet saw.'

'Why are you thinking about giving it all up? New York, everything? It's your whole life.'

They were sitting in the sun, watching tourists pass back and forth across the mediaeval bridge that Monet had painted. It joined the old and new sides of the hill village. The old town meandered upwards in a series of narrow passages and alleys.

'It *was* my whole life.' Jake scuffed his heel in the dust. 'I'm just … burned-out, maybe. I want something different now. Before she left, I made my mother a couple of promises …'

His stomach tightened as his breath caught. So casually, without any contrivance on his part, he had the opening he needed. He could explain everything, sitting here, in the sun, in this peaceful old town. And then watch Cassie's face grow cold and her smile fade, if he didn't get the words to come out right? Something spiky kicked in his gut. Too soon. It was too soon. He wasn't prepared, wasn't ready. *You need more time. Just a little more time.*

He looked down at his hands, resting on his knees, unable to meet the innocent enquiry in Cassie's eyes. His skin seemed to have thinned, leaving him shaky and … vulnerable? He straightened up fast, pushing himself to his feet and pulling Cassie with him. To his intense relief, the feeling of defencelessness receded. Where the hell had it come from anyway? He'd faced up to the biggest names in the City and on Wall Street, addressed conventions, chaired meetings. He'd never sacked a single worker without telling them, in person, the reasons for letting them go. He could surely explain himself to one woman in a way that she could forgive? He just needed that little extra time. That was all.

Cassie, taken by surprise at his abrupt movement, clutched at him to get her balance.

'Hey – I'm sorry.' Jake steadied her. With their bodies so close, it was the most natural thing in the world to put up her face to be kissed. Cassie held tight, forcing the feel and pressure of his mouth into her memory banks, even as her senses swam.

'Are we done for the day? Are you ready to go back to the villa or shall we find somewhere to eat?'

'Not back to the villa.' Something else that she wanted to put into those memory banks surfaced. 'Tonight I'd like to go dancing.'

Chapter Thirty-One

They found a small snug bar, near to the casino, with a live jazz combo and a tiny dance floor. Close in Jake's arms, moving lazily in time to the music, Cassie found past and present melding in her mind. His arms enfolded her. His heart beat steadily under her ear as she rested her head against his chest. Just like so many other times, when they'd circled slowly to the rhythm, oblivious to anything but each other. At seventeen she hadn't known how little time she had. Now she was going to hold onto every second. Even as bittersweet pain coursed through her, she felt a flash of hope. If Jake was staying in Bath ... Maybe there was a chance ...

And before that, there was the hunt for Benson. Nothing was going to happen before their dinner date tomorrow night in Menton.

'Coffee?'

'I'll make it.' Jake pulled Cassie against him to kiss her. 'Some time.'

'I'll do it.' She gave him a nudge. 'You go and put the lights on in the other room.'

When she carried the tray through and set it down, music was playing softly and the lamps were lit. Jake opened his arms and she went into them. His hands were on the straps of her dress.

'No.' she backed him towards the sofa, pushing him down onto it. 'Tonight it's my turn.' She felt his muscles tense, then relax. He lay back, watching her as she unbuttoned his shirt and reached for his zipper.

The coffee went cold on the table.

Jake lay awake, hands behind his head, staring into the darkness, listening to Cassie breathing softly beside him in the four-poster. Her scent, mixed with jasmine from the garden, threatened to ambush his thoughts. He hauled them back again.

He and Cassie had to talk. Downstairs, this evening – heat spiked through him at the memory – hadn't been a time for *any* conversation. But he had to make a time, and a place. Lunch tomorrow? A fancy restaurant somewhere?

Even as the thought came to him he rejected it, moving restlessly. Images of other carefully staged lunch dates floated in his memory. An expensive meal in a top grade restaurant, a good but not great wine, a lavish farewell gift, wrapped and waiting with the maitre d'. And a limo booked, to take the girl home afterwards. Alone.

Recollections crunched painfully in his mind. He had a rep in New York as a smooth operator. Somehow – and he didn't quite know how – that smooth had begun to look pretty shallow. With Cassie his brand of polish seemed to have run for the hills. Being with her was taking him dangerously close to the tongue-tied, fumbling kid he'd been at age nineteen. She could skewer him with one glance of those grey-green eyes – turn him inside out, so that he barely remembered what day it was. When they had that talk he didn't want to hurt her – nor make her mad, entertaining as that could be. Maybe they could take a picnic, somewhere quiet. He wondered if there were any paper plates in the kitchen. If Cass threw them at him, they wouldn't leave bruises.

Cassie flipped her sunglasses from the top of her head and stared down at the Villa Constanza. It was still early. The morning was cool and quiet, a suggestion of haze promising heat to come. She'd left Jake asleep, sprawled over most of the bed, and taken the path behind the villa to this small open vantage point. She needed to get her thoughts in order. The agitation – no, make that panic – of discovering herself in love with Jake was settling. Now she needed a few ground rules.

Rule One. Jake must not find out.

Rule Two. Jake must not find out.

Rule Three. Jake must not find out.

She gave a breathy laugh. A girl had her pride, however stupid her heart might be. There was no way she was going to betray any neediness. She'd known what she was getting into with McQuire. Hearts broken, while you wait. Getting hers done twice – by the same guy – that was complete carelessness.

She lifted her chin. She'd make her memories of Jake, as she'd promised herself, but that didn't mean giving up hope. Who said she had to get bent out of shape this time around? The heat between her and Jake could melt glaciers. And he was probably going to stay in Bath. No reason to think they couldn't become an item. Loving a guy who didn't love you back wasn't so good, but it wasn't so bad either. *Right this second there are probably millions of women in the world doing just that.* If there was a hollow in the centre of her heart, she'd find a way to live with it.

She couldn't expect something of Jake that he didn't know how to give. So she'd take what she could get. She'd rather have Jake in her life, without love, than learn to do without him all over again. Maybe in time—

She shut down that train of thought fast. No trips to the fool's paradise. She was a practical woman and this is how it was. She sniffed fiercely and swallowed down the tears that had unaccountably risen in her throat. She had her eyes open this time around. She would take whatever Jake was offering, on whatever terms he offered it – but she was damned if she was going to let him know it.

'A picnic?'

'You don't like the idea?'

'I didn't say that.' Cassie was staring suspiciously at him, eyes narrowed. 'You wouldn't have anything else in mind, would you? Besides eating?'

Jake's skin went cold and his thoughts stuttered. 'Like what?'

'Oh – you know ...' Cassie prompted. 'A girl, a boy, a rug on the grass?'

'Oh, yeah.' His thoughts came back into focus. 'I guess that *might* happen.'

'Good.' She gave him a blinding grin. 'You know, for a minute there I thought you had a guilty conscience about something.'

'Why would you think that? Jake asked carefully.

'Men always have something they *ought* to feel guilty about. Whatever it is, I forgive you,' Cassie offered generously. 'But we need to be back in time to prepare for that dinner in Menton tonight. It would be a good chance to plan our strategy.' She tilted her head. 'I like it. We can have some of that wonderful focaccia from the bakery, and that cheese we bought the other day. And olives. And peaches. There must be peaches. And wine. Something pink and very cold. I'll get the corkscrew, then we need to hit the market ...' She disappeared into the kitchen, still talking.

Jake leaned against the wall, conscious of the sweat gathering between his shoulder blades. *What the hell is the matter with you? How hard can it be to tell one woman the truth?*

He had to get this *done*.

Chapter Thirty-Two

'It's busy down here today.' Cassie craned out of the car window as Jake nosed along, searching for a parking spot near the baker's. 'Oh, look! That's why.' She gestured at a notice propped on an easel outside the largest of the restaurants in the street. 'Film Company. Hiring today.' There was already a line of people, laughing and chatting, snaking along the pavement and spilling into the road. 'Let me out. I want to see.'

'Cass! What is there to see?' Jake frowned as he rejected a space alongside a row of scooters that was a foot too short. He glanced towards her. 'It's just a crowd of people hoping to get famous. I doubt if George Clooney is hanging around anywhere.'

'I won't know until I get out! Go on, it won't take a minute. Go and find somewhere to park and come back for me. I'll meet you here. *Please.*' She widened her eyes beseechingly, controlling her grin as Jake tried to keep a straight face and found he couldn't.

'Okay, pest. As you asked so nicely.' He stopped the car so she could hop out. 'Don't sign any contracts without me seeing them first – and remember, as your manager I get thirty per cent.' Cassie stuck out her tongue and stepped back to let him pull away.

Jake headed the car out of the crowded street, glad of the chance to catch his breath for a moment. Alone. There was a disturbing hollow under his ribs. The knot he was going to have to unravel with Cass just kept getting bigger and bigger. He'd been all kinds of an idiot to let the honeymoon mistake go unchallenged. There'd been a whole bunch of new e-mails today. This time he'd trashed them all immediately. The only one he'd read before deleting was from Tony. His oldest friend was demanding to know, in very basic English, what the hell was going on. And threatening damage if Cassie got hurt. That was what friends were for – to keep you on the straight and narrow, and rearrange your face if you strayed. Thank God no one had gotten hold of Cassie's name yet.

On auto-pilot Jake registered a parking slot opening up in front of him and pounced on it. It was going to take him a while to get back to where he'd left Cassie. If George Clooney was down there, she had plenty of time to find him.

Left alone, Cassie wandered towards the chattering group, wondering if Mitch's wife was anywhere in the throng. All the glass doors of the restaurant were open to the street. At the head of the queue a man with a baseball cap was handing out forms and directing people towards a bank of tables.

'Listen up, folks – today we're recruiting for two crowd scenes. Just fill in your details and step over there to speak to one of my associates. Move along, please.'

Cassie laughed and shook her head as he offered her a form.

'No?' he queried. 'You sure? We've always got room for a pretty lady.' He grinned. 'Don't want to miss your chance to see yourself in a movie, now.'

'I'm a visitor. I don't know how much longer I'm

going to be in San Remo.' The thought sent a small cloud scudding across her horizon.

'Well, if you change your mind, we'll be here again tomorrow.'

'Thank you.' Cassie turned away, scanning the street behind her for signs of Jake. He'd been right, she thought, with a half smile. There wasn't much to see. Maybe she'd even tell him so. She moved out of the way as a fresh batch of hopefuls reached the head of the line to claim their forms. On the far side of the restaurant, away from the crush, two men were sitting at a table littered with papers, photographs and bottles of mineral water. Now *that* looked far more interesting. As Cassie edged closer, trying to distinguish their faces, a slight breeze lifted the corner of the red and white checked tablecloth. One of the water bottles wobbled ominously. Both men moved fast to save the paperwork from a soaking. As he scooped a handful of photographs out of danger, Cassie got a better look at the one sitting with his back to her.

She stopped dead, sucking in air sharply. The restaurant was shady, in contrast to the brightness of the street, and he was dressed now in jeans and an open-necked shirt, in place of a suit and tie, but Cassie had no doubt about his identity.

'Gerald Benson!'

It was out before she could stop it.

The man heard her. His head jerked up and he swung towards her. Cursing her clumsiness, Cassie stepped forward. There was nothing she could do now but confront him. She held out her hand. 'I didn't expect to see you here, Mr Benson. I thought you were planning a trip to Scotland.' He was out of his seat, ignoring her outstretched hand. The man on the other side of the table leaned forward, dark hair flopping over his face. 'Hi there, Miss, can we help you?'

'I just wanted a few words with Gerald here.'

'Gerald?' The man looked confused. 'I thought your name was Ryan?'

'It is. She's made a mistake ... at least, she hasn't, but—I can explain.'

'I think you'd better.' The dark-haired man narrowed his eyes. 'Hey – this isn't some divorce or paternity thing, is it? You know our shooting schedule is tight. If you've got personal issues you need to resolve ...' He shrugged. 'No offence, ma'am.' He dipped his head Cassie's direction.

'No! You've got it all wrong. Both of you. Please, I *can* explain.' Gerald/Ryan made a placating gesture to the dark-haired man before spinning back to Cassie. 'Look, you weren't supposed to know, but—It's ... Oh hell ... I'm an actor.' He pointed to the table. Cassie stared at the pictures spread out on the checked cloth. Publicity shots – an actor's professional portfolio. 'I was hired—Oh.' His expression stiffened into a weird mix of relief and alarm as he glanced over Cassie's shoulder.

'What the hell are *you* doing here?'

Cassie jerked around to see Jake, his face like thunder, striding towards them. She gaped from one man to the other. Jake ... and Benson. Together. Her chest went tight. 'You two know each other?'

The dark-haired man was on his feet, demanding to be told what was happening. No one took any notice. Jake turned towards Cassie. There was a flush across his cheekbones, but his eyes were set hard. 'Yes. Look, we need to talk.' He shoved a hand through his hair. 'But right now I want to know what this clown is doing here.'

'Mr McQuire. I know what you said, about a low profile, but this is a *film*, man – like it could be my big career break, right here in town.' Gerald/Ryan's handsome face creased in a grimace somewhere between guilt and determination. 'Just let me tie this up. *Please*. I'm this close. This close—' He held up his hand, fingers almost most overlapping. '—to getting the part—'

'Not if you're already contracted to somebody else,' the dark-haired man intervened. 'It seems to me you've got a *lot* of issues here, buster—'

'Will you keep quiet?' Jake snarled. 'His arrangement with me ended ten seconds ago. You can have him—'

'Jake!' Cassie's voice cut across the argument, surprising even her with its clarity. On the other side of the restaurant people were turning around to look, drawn by the loud voices. 'Just let me get this straight,' she ploughed on, in the face of three angry stares and with an icy lump in her chest. '*You* hired this man to impersonate Gerald Benson?'

'Yes.' Jake's voice grated. 'But you just heard me fire him.' Jake reached out to take Cassie's hand, but she stepped back, out of reach. 'Sweetheart, we need to go somewhere, to talk about this.' He cast a hunted look at the crowd at the other side of the restaurant. 'I know it seems ... strange, but ...'

Cassie stared at him. His mouth was moving but somehow she couldn't hear anything. The sound was fading and the words weren't making sense. Instead she was getting brief flashes of the past few days. Meeting

210

Benson – only he wasn't Benson, his name was Ryan. Snooping around the Chelsea apartment. The Villa Constanza. The Villa Verdi. Jake's face, smiling, grinning, laughing – at her. Playing her for a fool – a big joke. *Set up, set up, set up.*

Heedlessly she turned, eyes half blinded with tears that were *not* going to fall, blundering between the tables. She steadied herself and picked up speed. She had to get away. A fast glance over her shoulder showed her Jake, close behind. But Ryan the actor had grabbed his arm, holding him up.

In five paces she was into the milling crowd of would-be extras. The car. She had to find the car – but where? And she had no keys. And Jake would follow her, as soon as he shook loose from Ryan.

Raised voices, the sound of a scuffle and falling furniture drifted after her.

'Cassie!' Like a guardian angel Mitch's wife stepped in front of her, face alight. 'This is *so* cool!' She was waving a slip of paper. 'They just took me on, as an extra.' Her eyes were wide with excitement. 'Have you come to try your luck? Let me go and see—'

'No, please.' Cassie put a shaky hand on the woman's arm. 'Do you have your car here? Only I need to get back to the villa. Now.'

'Yes. Of course. Are you feeling okay?' The woman's face creased with concern. 'I'm parked just over there.'

Free of encumbrances at last, Jake broke through the crowd, heart racing. He dodged around a couple of chairs, stacked by the kerb, searching frantically.

And there she was … getting into a car further down the street. 'Cassie!' He put all the power he could muster behind her name.

She heard him. Her head came up. He caught a brief glimpse of her face, white and stricken, and then she ducked into the passenger seat and disappeared from view.

The vehicle pulled out and accelerated away before he could reach it.

Oh God! What a God-awful mess. He dug his hand into the pocket of his jeans, fishing for the car keys. He had to follow …

But the hire car was a mile away.

He stood still, suddenly cold. Something was trying to turn him to stone, from the heart outwards.

If he let Cassie go like this …

Then you might as well stop breathing.

The world swirled and went light, then dark, then cleared.

Finally, standing in the middle of a sunny Italian street, with people stepping around him, looking at him curiously, the other shoe dropped.

Now he got it. This was what his mother's second challenge had been about. The one he hadn't disclosed to anyone.

There was an ache in his chest like someone had stuck an ice-cold blade there.

He was hopelessly, devastatingly in love with Cassie Travers.

He turned and began to run.

Chapter Thirty-Three

Cassie held together long enough to thank Mitch's wife, before she almost fell out of the car. The headache she'd invented as an excuse was starting to throb for real.

The villa was mercifully quiet. Vitoria had left for the day. With no more need to restrain them, tears fell uncontrollably, making dark blotches on the pale pink of her blouse. Cassie made one attempt to wipe them away with the back of her hand, then gave up and let them come.

Tears and confusion had her breath hitching in short sobs as she raced up the stairs. She didn't have much time. She had to be out of here before Jake got back. Almost at the top of the stairs she staggered to a stop, holding the banister for support. Jake's sweater, discarded over the rail, pushed the sobs to a crescendo. She wanted to snatch it up, bury her face in it, inhale the familiar Jake scent, for comfort. *Comfort?*

With a jerk she forced her feet to move, throwing herself up the remaining stairs. This whole thing had been a sham: the villa, the London flat, Benson. She'd fallen for it, brushing aside every niggle of doubt. *Because you wanted to believe?* Jake had set it all up. He'd *hired* Benson. Why? A joke? Another bet? Some incomprehensible man thing? *Does it matter now?*

She reached her old room. Dragging her bag from under the bed she hauled it into the room with the four-poster. Turning her back on the bed with a shudder, she flung open the door of the wardrobe. And stopped dead.

Clothes, shoes, Jake had paid for all of them. She rammed her fist into her mouth to stop herself from howling. She couldn't take them. She didn't *want* them. Snatching up the few things she'd brought with her that were worth retrieving, her hand brushed the hem of the dress she'd worn to the casino. *That* dress.

Fresh tears rose in her throat as the memory of Jake's appreciative eyes arced into her mind. Then a sudden surge of fury wiped out the tears. With a sharp ripping movement she wrenched it off the hanger, screwed it into a ball and pitched it through the open window. It flew out like a comet.

Racing to the window to follow its descent, she watched it spread out and float gently down, to land in the pool. The bright colours of the silk blurred into each other, drifting on the blue water. Grabbing her handbag she opened her purse, emptying the contents on the bed. She had just enough euros for a taxi to the train station and a ticket to Nice. Then a bus, if she could find one, or another taxi. When she reached the airport ... *Worry about that when you get there.*

She crammed the money back into her bag. Moving through the room at a run, she shoved underwear, make-up, her favourite top, into the suitcase. The white jeans, still stained faintly pink despite Vitoria's best efforts, went in last.

Her hand was on the handle of the case when she heard the unmistakable sound of a car skidding to a halt on the gravel at the side of the house, followed by running footsteps. Jake! She cast a desperate look round, but there was no way out.

And what's the use of hiding?

She raised her chin, and squared her shoulders. She'd tough it out, with dignity. *At least this way you won't be looking over your shoulder, checking if he's behind you.*

She picked up the bag and strode out to the landing.

Heart in overdrive, Jake hurtled up the front steps, three at a time, bursting into the house.

'Cassie? Oh God!' Through the open salon door and the French windows he saw the pool. And the white mass floating in it. 'Cassie!'

'There's no need to yell.' From behind him her voice cut the air like a cool blade, finding unprotected skin. Wincing, he spun round and then stood still, gathering himself. She was coming down the stairs, her case in her hand.

'Cass, you can't go. *Please.*' Even in his own ears it sounded as if he was chewing gravel. The blade sliced deeper into him when he saw her tear-ravaged face. He swore, softly and bitterly.

'Don't get any ideas, McQuire.' She'd reached the bottom step. Her chin was high, with a pride that shredded his heart. 'There are tears of pain, and tears of anger. These—' She waved her hand. '—are tears of anger. Step aside please, and let me pass.'

'No.' He closed the distance between them. 'First you listen.' He knew his voice was unsteady. 'You want to leave then, I won't stop you.'

'I prefer to leave now. You can keep whatever it is you want to say to yourself.'

'Give me ten minutes. Just ten. Then ... if you still ...'

He shrugged helplessly. 'I'll drive you wherever you want to go.'

Cassie shook her head, her eyes still shiny with tears. 'Just let me go, please.'

'I can't. You have to hear me.' With no more strength and no defences left, Jake closed his eyes, then blinked them open. 'If you want me on my knees, you've got it.' He let himself down slowly, eyes riveted to her face. If she walked away now, left him kneeling there ...

Emotions roiled in Cassie's chest. Something totally and complacently feminine stretched sinuously inside her. He looked so cute, so lost, so—

Abruptly everything inside her stilled. Breath, thoughts, heart. She didn't want this. Whatever he'd done, she didn't want Jake on the floor in front of her, raw and vulnerable. And she couldn't walk away, leaving him there.

She might be an idiot, but she had to give him a chance. *Whatever he's done, you still love him.*

She dropped the case and sank to her knees, putting her hands on his shoulders. She could feel him trembling. Heard the throb in his voice as he whispered her name.

'I'm sorry, Cass. So sorry. I've been looking for a way to tell you.' His mouth twisted. 'I'm an asshole, for doing what I did, but there *was* a reason, and it wasn't to make a fool of you, if that's what you're thinking.' He gave a shaky laugh. 'The joke is on me. *I'm* the fool here. And if I lose you ...'

Barely knowing why, but knowing it was *right*, she leaned towards him. His lips met hers, tentative and hesitant.

Their mouths were hardly touching, but somehow she felt something shift, deep in her being. Somewhere in that lightest of touches the foundations of who Cassie Travers was changed forever.

This is coming home.

Between one heartbeat and the next Jake claimed her.

Surrender doesn't have to mean losing.

But there's still a road to travel.

They swayed apart. Jake looked punch-drunk, his eyes shadowed. Heaven alone knew how she looked.

He covered her hands with his own. 'Let me explain?'

She ran her tongue over her lip. 'Okay.'

She retreated, to perch on the bottom-most step of the stairs. Jake wrapped his arms around his knees, sitting on the tiled floor of the hall. His hair was rumpled, falling forward onto his face. He brushed it back impatiently. Cassie felt her heart stutter. He looked like the boy she'd loved at seventeen. The boy she'd never stopped loving. That *had* been love. And it had never gone away. Not completely.

She drank him in as he visibly sorted his thoughts, eyes closed and face strained. Strength was flowing through her. She could do this. The ties between them had gone underground in her heart, but hadn't broken. Even so—

She stuck out a foot and nudged his leg. 'Come on, McQuire, get it done. It had better be good. Or I'm out of here.' At the tone of her voice some of the tension leached out of his face. He opened his eyes and smiled.

That smile. The toe-curling one.

Oh hell. You've got it bad, girl.

She wasn't about to let him know it, but she really

wasn't going anywhere. Not for the next fifty years or so. After that she'd review. If McQuire objected, he'd just have to learn to live with it.

'I think …' he began, leaning forward. 'It goes back to when I left for New York. My dad … He was a stranger, but I was dazzled, Cass. He had such power. Charisma, I suppose.' *Like father, like son*, Cassie thought, composing her face encouragingly. 'I left Bath, and I didn't look back. He came for me because he'd decided he wanted an heir. And he always got what he wanted. Ma … maybe she realised then what would happen, but she didn't do or say anything – just told me to take my opportunities wherever they offered. I was thinking holiday, a little bonding time with a father I'd barely even met … I don't know.' He dug his hand in his hair. 'Truth is, I probably didn't think at all. The weeks passed, then it was months … Everything was so different. There was so much to learn, to be.' Cassie heard the wonder in his voice. 'Bath seemed … old, slow, ordinary. And a long way away.' He shifted slightly. 'You weren't the only one I abandoned, Cassie. It was my mother too. She never stood in my way, never tried to get me back, and I must've hurt her, the same way I hurt you.'

Cassie shrugged, finding her throat threatening to close on a different sort of tears.

'My father taught me the business, gave me more and more responsibility, groomed me to succeed him. Then he died. He'd had the heart condition for a while. That was probably why he came looking … And then it was all mine. But … I don't know …' He stopped. Cassie waited. 'Gradually, over the years, things began to change. In me. I didn't get the buzz any more. I was wired all the time, but it didn't have that same feeling. Some of my father's business methods ... Well, they began to look a little too sharp, too careless about the people who worked for him. I told myself I was suffering from burn-out, I took a vacation ... I tried booze ...' He hesitated. 'And sex. Nothing did it for me. There was only one thing to do, one way to go. I started to downshift. Couldn't think of anything else ... and it seemed to be working. I let the smaller holdings go first, encouraged the staff to buy me out, merged or sold a few others ... Then I found out that Ma was seriously ill. She didn't tell me how bad it was, Cass. Didn't want to spoil my life.' His eyes were almost black with painful recollection. 'It was left to Tony to tell me that my mother might be dying.' The laugh he gave had no humour in it. 'He told me to haul my sorry ass back to Bath if I wanted to spend some time with her before it was too late. It was like ... I'd woken from a spell, or something. I handed the running of everything but the core company, McQuire Projects, to my vice presidents and I shipped home. Ma was in the hospital. She never reproached me, never asked ...' His voice shuddered. 'It was life- threatening. They never concealed that. But it was treatable, and she responded. And when she was back on her feet and had decided that she wanted to see something of the world ...' His mouth softened in a reflective grin that had Cassie's fragile heart pooling at her feet.

'She didn't pry, but one day she just asked, out of the blue, if there was anyone special that I'd left behind in New York. Of course there wasn't, but then we got talking about the girls I'd dated. She was teasing me about it and somehow, I don't know how, she challenged me – dared

219

me – I don't know which, to run her business and to date what she called "a real girl", like someone I met through work, or something. One thing led to another and next I knew I'd taken a bet about running the business *and* dating that real girl. She'd got me right where she wanted me. She was laughing all the way to the damn cruise ship.'

Cassie's confusion was dropping away. '*I* was the real girl. Should I be flattered, McQuire, or insulted?' She wrinkled her nose, unable to decide. 'But the Benson charade?'

Jake shifted uncomfortably, not quite meeting her eyes. 'Ma talked about someone I worked with, or met through work. At first I couldn't think how that would happen. There wasn't any one I worked with that I wanted to date. Then Bennie let slip that you were in financial trouble and might lose the business and I remembered a few things, about you and me …' Now he did look up, to meet her eyes. 'Once I'd had the idea … It had to be you, Cass. No one else would do. I guess that should have told me something, even then. I pumped Tony for more information about you and about the business and he confirmed the impression I had from Benita: that you had zero interest in me – the past was the past and you'd moved on.'

'And, of course, that made me even more of a challenge,' Cassie said drily.

'Of course,' he agreed. 'I angled a bit, but Bennie was clear you wouldn't want to meet me. She actually opened up and told me that you were pretty scathing on the subject. Which I didn't quite understand, *then*. Getting you to go out with me obviously would have taken forever – assuming you'd even agree to see me in the first place. I was impatient. I wanted to hurry things along. I needed to do what Ma wanted, even though it seemed so crazy – but it still had to be on my terms. I couldn't let go of that much control. So the Benson thing was born. You went for it.' His mouth twisted wryly. '*Really* went for it. I should have known you never do anything by halves. And then everything got *way* out of control. I was stupid in that too. I hadn't thought beyond the stuff in London. *That* was all set up to run like clockwork, but there was no forward plan at all. I did arrange in advance for that guy Ryan to fly in yesterday, in case I needed him for something at the restaurant tonight, but that was all. And you saw how that worked out. ' He held up his hands. 'Once we got here, I expected it to be just like a holiday – Why I imagined that you'd suddenly give up on the idea of chasing Benson ...' He shook his head in disbelief. 'I've been improvising like crazy ever since we arrived. Running all over, setting up that stuff at the Villa Verdi, and keeping you away from the place until I had it organised. *And* away from the laptop. The day of the party I had information on 'Benson' ready to show you. Then I realised that if you did any kind of search for yourself, you'd soon find out something was wrong. Those few seconds by the pool took ten years off my life, I swear.'

'You bought me off with ice-cream,' she recollected. 'And then sabotaged the machine? Nice to know I kept you on the hop.' She took a second to savour a flicker of revenge. 'Benson was just an actor.'

'As you discovered. There is a Gerald Benson, but not the one you met. The genuine one works for my London office.'

'And the apartment in Chelsea?'

'Belongs to McQuire Projects. Gerald manages it, amongst other things. We use it to put up executives visiting London.' He answered her raised eyebrows. 'Not me, I always stay at Claridge's.'

'That figures.' She frowned. 'What about Carl – the security man?'

'He was *not* meant to happen. Just a guy doing his job. Can't say I was unhappy at the result though.'

'Hmm.' Cassie refused to be drawn. 'Who left the message in Italian on the answer-phone?'

'A friend in Milan. He still doesn't know what the heck it was all about.'

Cassie let out a long breath. 'I didn't stand a chance did I?' she said, shaking her head. 'Why did you choose the Riviera?'

'Bennie said you thought Fairbrook might be here, so there was a chance of tracking down your money. I didn't expect him to walk into our arms though. The Riviera suited me, I wanted somewhere glamorous – that you would think was romantic. *Then* you'd have the opportunity to rediscover how irresistible I am.'

Cassie narrowed her eyes. 'Still trying to impress me, huh? I suppose the honeymoon thing was all in the interests of romance?'

Jake shook his head and skidded across the floor, to put a hand on Cassie's knee. 'I promise you, the honeymoon mess-up was just that, a mess-up. But that's got out of control too.' He pulled in a deep breath. 'I think you're going to have to marry me, Slick.'

Chapter Thirty-Four

'Marry you!' Cassie nearly hopped off the stairs. Her heart tried to push her ribs out of the way, to get out through her chest. 'I haven't said yet that I'll even *forgive* you, McQuire! Why do I have to marry you? We always took precautions, even that night on the antique sofa, so you can't be pregnant.'

Marriage? To Jake? The idea had her heart bouncing from throat to stomach and back again. A bit like seasickness.

'Everyone thinks I'm married,' Jake explained. 'I have all these e-mails and texts congratulating me. Plus that piece in the paper. It's going to be horrendous to unpick.'

'It's always about you, isn't it, McQuire? As I recall, no one has ever mentioned my name. Seems to me *you're* the one with the problem.' She couldn't stop the grin, didn't even try. He looked so cute when he was harassed. Tormenting him was too easy, and too much fun, before she let him down gently. Her breath stuttered a little at that thought.

'You don't know the half of it.' He groaned and dropped his head in his hands. 'Tony is going to come after me and hurt me if I don't.'

Even cuter. Despite that stutter, Cassie giggled, putting her hand to her mouth. Jake's head jerked up. 'Hey! He's very protective of you. Italian genes. Wife's BFF. Little sister he never had. I tell you, I'm toast. The shotgun is already loaded. If I don't want a butt full of pellets, I've got to do the right thing.'

The right thing. Cassie stared at him, a jag of pain scoring its way through the laughter. She looked him over, suddenly sober. Marriage was definitely on the table. No question. Shock juddered through her. *Now how the heck did that happen?*

The right thing. And there was so much that *was* right ... Forget that stupid idea of a man she could mould the way she wanted. Jake ... Jake was ... everything she could ever need. They laughed, they fought, heck – they even cooked together. His body was hers for the taking. She knew exactly where and how to touch him to reduce all that mind and muscle to gloop – well, except for one important part. *You* could *marry this man.*

But he hadn't said it. The 'L' word. She could manage without it though, couldn't she? If she had to? If she had all the rest? *Do you want to marry Jake McQuire?*

He was leaning back, arms braced behind him on the floor. All trace of humour had drained away from his face. A second ripple of shock flashed through Cassie. He looked gaunt and wide open, as if *she* had something he was desperate for.

'Jake?' she said uncertainly.

'I don't know if you want to hear this. If this is the time. But I have to say it. I love you.'

'What!' Air got twisted in her throat as she tried to breathe.

'I love you.'

'S ... since when?' The floor seemed to be shifting. Cassie put a hand to the banister to hold herself steady.

'Since this morning. That's when I realised. When I saw you getting in that car. I thought I'd blown it.' He gazed at her, helplessly. 'I don't know what else it can be. That challenge of my mother's, about a real girl – she wouldn't tell me what was supposed to come next – said I should wait to find out. I couldn't figure it out. She keeps sending me texts, asking whether I've cottoned on yet.' He shook his head disbelievingly. 'I couldn't even make a guess. I must have been blocking it. Now I know. I love you, Cassandra Maude Travers, and I can't live without you. I know I might have a way to go before you forgive me and maybe you want to think a bit, make me suffer probably.' He forestalled her as she opened her mouth to speak. 'But I'm not going to take no, if it's your first answer. I reckon if we work together a bit more, then you'll get used to the idea that I'm going to be around.' There was a determined light in his eyes now. 'I'm going to make you trust me.'

'You can start by forgetting I ever told you what my full name is.' Cassie fought to keep her face straight and her wildly swooping emotions in check. Any moment now something was going to burst, but before that …

Suffer. He'd said suffer. Just a bit, for just a little while. Didn't she deserve that much? 'While you're working on my trust issues, what are we going to do about the marriage thing?' She made it as casual as she could. 'When we get back to Bath? And everybody starts asking questions? If we're not actually married. Or even living together and all that stuff?'

He frowned. 'Well – you could move in with me.'

She shook her head. 'Not sure about that.'

'Well – I suppose it would have to look like we'd broken it off. Until I can persuade you.' For a second his eyes looked desolate. 'Maybe we could stage a stand-up fight, somewhere good and public—'

'I like that one.'

Jake ignored the interruption. 'You announce that it's all over, but I don't take no for an answer ...' He sighed. 'I'd prefer a quick trip to Vegas to tie the knot, no questions asked. Are you sure you couldn't take a chance?'

'Elvis wedding chapel?'

'If you want.' His chest rose and fell as he breathed deep. She could watch it all day – well, for an hour or two.

'Mmm.' She pretended to consider. 'It's tempting, but I don't think so. You know, I'm sure we could just laugh it off and go on as we have been. I've enjoyed working with you. I can always find an opening for a reliable member of staff. How much do you know about butlers?'

'I presume you mean about being one, rather than employing one? I have to say it's never been in my career plan.' He sat up and scooted closer, to capture her hand, looking down at it thoughtfully. 'Of course, you have been wearing my rings for almost a week now.'

'I ... what?' Wide-eyed, Cassie jerked her hand out of his grip, to examine the gold band and the cluster of rubies and diamonds. She could it see, now. The way they glinted in the light. There was a strange sinking feeling somewhere in her middle. 'They're real, aren't they?'

Jake nodded. 'I got them in Bond Street. I was expecting you to jump at the chance of wearing them – not make me force them onto your finger.' He looked rueful, then anxious. 'If you'd rather something else, we can change them.'

'Um.' She stared at the engagement ring, sparkling up at

her. Real rubies and real diamonds. 'You don't do things by halves either, do you, McQuire?' She slanted a glance up. 'This fight, the very public one that we might have. Would I get to scream, and throw things?'

His face had gone a little pale. 'If you must.'

'Where would we do it? The bar in one of the big hotels? The foyer of the theatre? Outside the Roman Baths?' she mused. Jake had gone from pale to paler. Suddenly she couldn't tease him any more. 'No.' She shook her head. 'I think I like the other idea better. The carry on as we have been, I mean.'

'Cass—'

She raised a hand to stop him speaking, looking into his eyes. 'Except that I do want these rings to be the real deal.'

'Real deal?' Jake had his head tilted towards her. His body was tense, the frown back in place, but now there was something in his eyes she recognised. Hope. 'Are you saying what I think you're saying? You don't just want to work together? You're asking me to marry you?'

'You know how I always like to call the shots.' She put her hand flat on his chest and felt his heart thumping against her fingers. It was beating for her now. She cleared her throat of the huskiness that had abruptly gathered there. 'I love you, Jake.' She sighed. 'I'm not sure that I ever stopped.' She dropped her hand and sat back. 'You asked me the other night who was the guy who did the number on me.' She waited, and saw when realisation hit.

'Oh God! Cassie—'

She gestured for silence, and he subsided, biting his lip.

'Trusting you isn't just about the Benson scam, Jake. You hurt me before, when you left Bath to go with your

father. You said it was just for a few weeks ... I waited ...'
She blinked. 'I thought then that you were my future. You
were my whole world – which was probably pretty stupid
of me. No one should put that kind of expectation on
another human being – but I was seventeen and in love for
the first time.' *And for the last time too?* 'I couldn't believe
that you weren't coming back, that you'd really left me.'
She swallowed. 'It took a while, but I finally understood.
You didn't feel the same way about me as I did about you,
and about what we had together. What I *thought* we had.
Something died inside me then ... when I finally realised
that you'd gone for good. I'd trusted you. It was my trust
that died.' *Which is why there's never really been anyone
else. Even when you hoped you were falling in love with
Jason, you never took that final step ...* 'I love you.' She
looked down at the ring, glittering on her finger. Jake's
ring. *And it isn't too late. It really isn't.* 'I love you, but
I still have those trust issues around you.' She flashed a
warning with her eyes as he made to interrupt. 'But I'm
prepared to work on them. You can have your chance,
Jake. Make me trust you.'

Relief erupted through Jake's veins. He surged to his feet,
pulling Cassie with him. 'I can do it, believe me. You're
never going to regret this, I swear. I'm going to spend the
rest of my life making you happy.'

His heart flipped hard against his ribs, as she looked up
at him, and smiled.

'I think I can settle for that.'

Jake's killer smile heated Cassie's skin as he bent his head.

Then she was pressed so tightly to him that she didn't have breath to speak. Or brain-power to think. She clung to him when the kiss finally broke. Jake put his hands to the sides of her head, tipping it back so that he could look at her. A tiny cloud of uncertainty still hovered. 'You did mean it?'

'That I love you, or that I want to marry you?'

'Both.'

'Well, I seem to be stuck with the love thing. The marriage?' She shrugged. 'You're a bossy, argumentative, control freak – but you also have a very cute rear end.' She reached round to pat it approvingly. 'I don't want to think of Tony peppering it with lead shot, so we'll just have to go through with it.' She stood on tiptoe and kissed his mouth.

He wrapped his arms around her and held her close. 'Do you want some huge thing in Bath Abbey, with a dozen bridesmaids trailing after you?'

'No!' She shook her head violently. 'Can we just go to that amazing marriage room in Menton and do it? Post the bans and get Benita and Tony over, for witnesses or whatever?'

'I'll go and ring them now.' He found her mouth again. 'Or maybe later.'

A long while later Cassie sat up in bed, looking thoughtfully at the open door of the wardrobe and the empty hanger lying on the floor. 'Jake?' She ran a finger down warm, bare skin, revelling in the texture. And the heady shot of love and desire that kicked in her blood as she felt Jake's quiver of reaction. He rolled over and squinted up at her, hair flopping into his eyes.

'Yes – I still love you. Come here.' He opened his arms.

'I still love you too.' Cassie snuggled up. 'But that wasn't what I wanted to know.' He was kissing the back of her neck. 'Get off! That tickles.' She gave him a shove. 'This is serious.'

'All right.' He sat up, and leaned away, with a long-suffering sigh. 'What do you want?'

Cassie gave him her widest smile. 'Can I borrow your credit card to buy a wedding dress?'

Epilogue

The Riviera, late autumn

The sun sparkled on blue water. A light breeze ruffled the leaves of the palm trees. Cassie's heart soared with the sunshine. It was *her* day. Hers and Jake's. Jake's hand was warm in hers. Their steps matched as they walked along the Menton seafront. It was a glorious day for late autumn.

And they were being followed.

The giggles and whispers, in mingled accents of French, English and American approached and receded as the group of teenage girls moved closer, then hung back if she or Jake showed any sign of turning around. A game of grandmother's footsteps with a very specific quarry. Words and phrases fluttered back and forth.

'Les fleurs.'

'Wedding …'

'… who's next …?'

Jake looked down at her, grinning. 'I think they're waiting for you to throw the bouquet.'

Cassie laughed. 'I got that too.' Even if she hadn't been carrying the tightly furled posy of white and cream rose buds in her hand, the ochre lace of the Jenny Packham dress, flipping around her calves, not to mention the flowers in her hair, suggested the presence of a wedding in her recent past. She'd handed over her antique lace veil to Benita for safekeeping but kept the roses twined in her up-swept hair.

Look, I mean, flowers. *Like how often does a serious business woman get to wear flowers in her hair?*

The stalkers were getting bolder. The giggles were louder.

'How about it? Are you going to give them what they want?' Jakes slanted a look down at her.

'Why not?' She swung their joined hands in the air. 'Let's do it.'

Laughing, Jake grabbed her under the arms, lifting up on to a low wall beside the sea, and holding her hand to keep her balance. The stalkers immediately gathered in front of her in a shifting, excited group, jostling, laughing and catcalling. Cassie shut her eyes, took a deep breath, and threw the flowers high in the air.

Scuffling, more giggling, then a collective 'Ahhhh!'

Cassie opened her eyes again and burst out laughing, leaning against Jake's shoulder.

The bouquet hadn't been snatched out of the air, as she expected. Instead it had landed neatly in the lap of an elderly lady sitting on a bench behind the group of girls. Madame's silver-haired beau, seeing his cue with evident delight, slid off the bench beside her and down on one knee, hands clasped over his heart. His lady was laughing, blushing, hiding her face in the flowers. Gently he reached out to take her hand, prompting her to look up.

There was a second of breathless stillness. Then a brisk emphatic nod of the head. 'Oui.'

All the watchers cheered, as the happy bridegroom-to-be kissed his new fiancée. Cassie nudged Jake and he swung her down from the wall, stealing his own kiss before setting her on her feet. Warmth and happiness shivered over her skin.

Perfect day.

The enterprising owner of a cafe across the street emerged, clutching a bottle of champagne. Jake caught the man's eye, signalling that he would pay. After a brief consultation glasses appeared and were handed round, and the popping of corks and the fizz of soda cans added to the celebration.

'Well, that was a surprise.'

'But a good one.' Cassie tilted her head to look up at her new husband, as they resumed their stroll along the promenade. The newly engaged couple's families, hastily summoned by text, the patrons of the cafe, several passers-by and a crowd of teenage boys, who had emerged from the shadows once it was clear that they were safe from the effects of flying bouquets, had turned the celebration into an impromptu party. Cassie wondered if Jake had ever had his hand shaken or his back slapped quite so many times in the space of two hours. She was sure she had never been kissed so often by complete strangers. Congratulations had become even more fervent when it was established that Jake was the one footing the bill.

Grinning, Jake let go of her hand, drawing her instead against his side. 'Happy Mrs McQuire?'

'Yes, Mr McQuire.' Cassie let out a long, contented sigh, laughing as Jake navigated her around two elderly ladies with attendant poodles. 'You know what? I could really get used to living here.'

'Is that a hint?'

'No!' Cassie dug her elbow into Jake's ribs. 'You might recall that I have a growing business to run.'

'Argh!' Jake pretended to be winded. 'And you just promised to love and cherish me. Remember that?'

'Later.' Cassie batted her eyelashes. If any more happiness bubbled in her chest, she was going to burst. *Who would have guessed that being married to Jake McQuire could make you feel like this?*

'Promises.' Jake cuddled her closer. 'You know now that you can run the business successfully without always being in Bath – you've proved that while we've been here, satisfying all the pre-requirements for the wedding.'

Cassie shot him a dark look. 'Once I was able to plough back the money that Slimeball Jason stole. *And* I had a *reliable* Internet connection.'

Wisely, Jake just grinned.

He knows I can't resist that look, dammit.

Cassie stuck out her tongue. Jake crossed his eyes and they only narrowly avoided colliding with a man leading two pugs. They walked on, hands enmeshed. She'd loved the time they'd spent here on the Riviera, waiting for all the formalities to be complete. She wanted to come back often, now that she knew that they could.

They were getting closer to the marina. Out at sea a sleek white yacht stood at anchor, with a handful of smaller boats bobbing around it.

'I take it you do have somewhere in mind for us to spend the night?' Cassie asked. They'd given Benita and Tony the keys to the apartment in Menton that they'd been renting, so that they could use it for the remainder of the wedding weekend. 'Or should we have staked out one of those benches, back there?'

'All under control. In fact, I think we've arrived.'

Within a few minutes Jake was handing her into a waiting motor launch. The two-man crew cast off, and then they were flying over the water.

'Oh!' It took only a second for Cassie to work it out. They were heading for the big white yacht.

It was even bigger when they pulled up alongside.

Cassie was pleased with the way she navigated herself on board, lace dress and all. The moment Jake's feet hit the deck behind her, he swept her up into his arms.

'What are you doing?' Cassie started to wriggle.

'Stop that! The bride has to be carried over the threshold.'

'You sentimental old thing, you.' Delighted, she nuzzled his neck so he wouldn't see.

'Hey! Not so much of the old.'

He carried her to the stern of the boat. A small table was set out, with more champagne and a tray of delicious looking nibbles. Settled in a chair, with a glass in her hand, Cassie had the chance of taking in her surroundings. She sensed, rather than saw, a bustle of preparation around them. Very soon they would be on their way. A shiver ran through her. Sailing into the unknown. *With Jake.*

'Are you cold?' He'd picked up on the shiver.

'No. Just a bit ...' She shrugged.

'A momentous day.' Something inside her shifted when she saw the understanding in his face. *This is your life, now.* 'I love you, Mrs McQuire.'

The dark blue eyes focused on her face. *I could drown in those eyes.*

In fact she *was* drowning. Out of the clear blue sky, a hot spike of anguish rocked through her.

What have I done?

She looked round hastily. 'I ... You didn't have to ... we could have ... Hiring something like this.' She stopped, eyes widening. 'No. Not hired. You *own* it.'

Jake was watching her over the rim of his glass. 'Don't panic, Cass.' He put out his hand to capture hers. The brush of his skin pulsed along her nerve endings. 'I'm not trying to swamp you. It *is* our honeymoon.' He smiled slowly, easily. His fingers were warm and familiar. The strange surge of apprehension began to abate and the tightness in Cassie's chest dialled down a fraction. 'We might as well get something out of the way now. Which side do you want? Port or starboard?'

Cassie stared at him. Confusion was replacing apprehension. 'What do you mean?'

'As of—' Jake squinted down at his watch, then gave up trying to calculate with a shrug. '—a number of hours ago, half of this totally decadent monster belongs to you. Half of all my worldly goods belong to you.' He put down his glass, took both her hands in his, and leaned forward. 'And all of me.'

A small dam inside Cassie burst suddenly. Her eyes were gritty, but she was *not* going to cry. 'Oh, Jake.'

'Come here.' He pulled her to her feet and onto his lap, holding her close. She cuddled her head against his shoulder. 'It's not a trap, Cassie, it's freedom. I promise.' He tilted his head back to look at her, raising her chin with his hand. 'I'm not stupid enough to imagine that exchanging rings means that we will sail into the sunset and everything will be perfect from now on. We will fight. You will throw things. I will duck. We will have fantastic make-up sex. It's life, Cass. It's what I want with you.'

'Jake.' All she seemed to be able to do was say his name. She leaned her face closer to his. The kiss was soft and sweet, with a thread of heat that trapped her breath.

When they moved apart Jake gave her a teasing grin. 'Of course, if you absolutely, totally and completely hate the yacht, then we'll have to go back and find that bench.'

'Idiot!' She feathered a kiss at the edge of his mouth and was gratified when his arms wrapped even more securely around her. 'I had a little wobble. Thanks for dealing with it.'

'No thanks necessary. I kind of thought you might, but I wasn't expecting it today, at least ...'

An undercurrent in his voice made her sit up to stare at him. 'Jake McQuire, did you think I'd get cold feet, and back out of the wedding?'

'Crossed my mind, the way I set you up. No.' He put a finger over her lips when she began to protest. 'I told you I wanted to make it up to you for the Benson thing. I *need* to. I want to make you happy, Cass. I know your work makes you happy, it's part of who you are. But I hope that you'll be able to keep on growing the concierge business and taking on staff, so it's not always you that has to do *everything*. I've never really thought about it before, but I'd like us to have a family.'

Family. Cassie had a sudden vision of their own

miniature Prince Harry look-alike, with her red hair and Jake's height and strong jaw. Or a little girl, with Jake's dark hair and blue eyes.

'Yes.' She breathed in, slowly. 'I'd like that too.'

'Well, we have plenty of scope to practise.' His smile tilted towards wicked. He kissed her again. *A lot more heat.* He rested his forehead against hers. 'We'll work it out, my love, I promise.' He eased back. 'I haven't had a serious talk to Ma about the business yet, seeing as how she's never home these days—' Mrs McQuire senior had come back from her cruise on the arm of a younger man, who was currently helping her make up for lost time, by whisking her from one exotic destination to another. '—but I'd like to take over Kings, officially, if she agrees.' His eyes glittered with provocation. 'Maybe I should have asked her today? She was in a real good mood, knowing how her thing with the bet worked out.' He raised his eyebrows. 'If she's willing for me to buy her out, could you live with a full-time detective?'

Cassie pretended to consider it. 'A sexy detective?'

'Of course!'

'Then I think I could give it a go.' She ran her finger around one of the buttons on his very simple, very expensive, white silk shirt. The idea of unbuttoning it was sending quivers of anticipation through her, but this was exciting too. *The future. Their future.* 'We could bring the two businesses together, offices in the same building.' Her imagination had started to roll.

'Never mind the same building, let's make it one each. Adjoining. With a top floor office each.'

'And a connecting door between them?'

Jakes eyes glinted. 'I want a *very* big desk. Substantial.' The heat in his look was making her toes tingle.

She dropped her eyes demurely to hide the answering glint. 'And I've always wanted an office with a chaise longue in it, one of those pretty antique ones.'

'A French chaise longue?' Jake sat up, with her in his arms. 'Tomorrow we scour every antique shop in Nice.' The kiss was long and deep and very satisfying.

Cassie wound her arms around Jake's neck as he carried her to the rail and set her on her feet. Menton was receding fast as the boat headed out along the coast.

'Nice? Is that where we will be tomorrow?'

'Tomorrow, yes. After that – wherever you like. We've got the world, Cassie. We'll make this thing work. We've got a future.'

Cassie turned in Jake's arms, leaning back against him to watch the boat's wake, stretching out in a wide white arc behind them. He pulled her close against his chest. The sun was sinking fast towards the horizon. Cassie ran her finger against the gold band on the third finger of her left hand.

Your first night as Mrs Jake McQuire.

And after that, the future.

'Is there a cabin in this monster with our name on?'

Jake nodded, stealing a kiss that lingered into something deeper. 'I think it is a distinct possibility.'

'In that case …' She stepped out of his arms to take his hand. 'Shall we go and find it?'

Thank You

Hello

This book was a new departure for me, as I usually write romantic suspense – books with a dark love story mixed with a scary thriller, and some super-nasty villains. This time it was fun to have the chance to explore my lighter side, writing a book full of summer sunshine. I really hope you enjoyed reading Cassie and Jake's story as much as I enjoyed writing it. I haven't given up on the romantic suspense though. I still like to indulge my dark side.

Fingers crossed I will be writing more of both kinds of book for Choc Lit, and that *Summer in San Remo* will be the first of a series – The Riviera Rogues – glamorous settings, romance, independently minded heroines and Choc Lit's essential ingredient, an irresistible hero.

One of the ways in which a reader can let an author know that they have enjoyed meeting the characters in a book, and that they would like to read more, is to write a review.

Authors love to have reviews. (So do their publishers. And the more stars, the better!)

Now that you've finished *Summer in San Remo*, could you take a few moments to write a review and post it online, to tell the world what you thought of it?

If you can tell your family, your friends and your book group, that's good too.

Thank you so much for reading *Summer in San Remo*.

See you again on the Riviera to catch up with Cassie and Jake's new life together, and to meet another romantic Riviera Rogue?

Evonne

About the Author

Evonne Wareham was born in South Wales and spent her childhood there. After university she migrated to London, where she worked in local government, scribbled novels in her spare time and went to the theatre a lot. Now she's back in Wales, living by the sea, writing and studying for a PhD in history. She still loves the theatre, likes staying in hotels and enjoys the company of other authors through her membership of both the Romantic Novelists' Association and the Crime Writers' Association

Evonne's debut novel, *Never Coming Home* won the 2012 Joan Hessayon New Writers' Award, the 2013 Colorado Romance Writers' Award for Romantic Suspense, the Oklahoma National Readers' Choice Award for Romantic Suspense plus was a nominee for a Reviewers' Choice Award from RT Book Reviews. Her second romantic suspense novel, *Out of Sight Out of Mind*, was a finalist for the Maggie Award for Excellence, presented by the Georgia Romance Writers' chapter of the Romance Writers of America.

www.twitter.com/evonnewareham
www.evonneonwednesday.blogspot.com

More Choc Lit

From Evonne Wareham

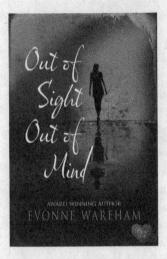

Out of Sight Out of Mind

Everyone has secrets. Some are stranger than others.

Madison Albi is a scientist with a very special talent – for reading minds. When she stumbles across a homeless man with whom she feels an inexplicable connection, she can't resist the dangerous impulse to use her skills to help him.

J is a non-person – a vagrant who can't even remember his own name. He's got no hope, until he meets Madison. Is she the one woman who can restore his past?

Madison agrees to help J recover his memory, but as she delves deeper into his mind, it soon becomes clear that some secrets are better off staying hidden.

Is J really the man Madison believes him to be?

Never Coming Home

Winner of the 2012 New Writers' Joan Hessayon Award

All she has left is hope.

When Kaz Elmore is told her five-year-old daughter Jamie has died in a car crash, she struggles to accept that she'll never see her little girl again. Then a stranger comes into her life offering the most dangerous substance in the world: hope.

EVONNE WAREHAM

Devlin, a security consultant and witness to the terrible accident scene, inadvertently reveals that Kaz's daughter might not have been the girl in the car after all.

What if Jamie is still alive? With no evidence, the police aren't interested, so Devlin and Kaz have little choice but to investigate themselves.

Devlin never gets involved with a client. Never. But the more time he spends with Kaz, the more he desires her – and the more his carefully constructed ice-man persona starts to unravel.

The desperate search for Jamie leads down dangerous paths – to a murderous acquaintance from Devlin's dark past, and all across Europe, to Italy, where deadly secrets await. But as long as Kaz has hope, she can't stop looking …

Available in paperback from all good bookshops and online stores. Visit www.choc-lit.com for details.

What Happens at Christmas

Kidnapped for Christmas?

Best-selling author Andrew Vitruvius knows that any publicity is good publicity. His agent tells him that often, so it must be true. In the run-up to Christmas, she excels herself – talking him into the craziest scheme yet: getting himself kidnapped, live on TV.

But when the plan goes ahead and Drew is unceremoniously thrown in the back of a van before being dragged to a hut in middle of the Brecon Beacons, it all starts to feel a little bit *too* real.

Meanwhile, not far away, Lori France and her four-year-old niece Misty are settling in to spend the holidays away after unexpected events leave them without a place to stay. Little do they know they're about to make a shocking discovery and experience a Christmas they're not likely to forget …

Available as an eBook on all platforms.
Visit www.choc-lit.com for details.

More from Choc Lit

If you enjoyed Evonne's story, you'll enjoy the
rest of our selection. Here's a sample:

Too Damn Nice
Kathryn Freeman

Do nice guys stand a chance?

Nick Templeton has been in
love with Lizzie Donavue for
what seems like forever. Just
as he summons the courage to
make his move, she's offered a
modelling contract which takes
her across the Atlantic to the
glamorous locations of New
York and Los Angeles. And far
away from him.

Nick is forced to watch from the sidelines as the gawky
teenager he knew is transformed into Elizabeth Donavue:
top model and the ultimate elegant English rose pin-up,
seemingly forever caught in a whirlwind of celebrity parties
with the next up-and-coming Hollywood bad boy by her
side.

But then Lizzie's star-studded life comes crashing down
around her, and a nice guy like Nick seems just what she
needs. Will she take a chance on him? Or is he too damn
nice?

Little Teashop of Horrors

Jane Lovering

Secrets, lies, carrot cake – and an owl called Skrillex!

Amy Knowles has always been the plain sidekick to her pretty best friend Jules. And whilst the tearoom they both work in on the Monkpark Hall estate in Yorkshire is not exactly awash with eligible bachelors, it's obvious where the male attention is concentrated – and it's not just on the cakes!

There is one man who notices Amy. Joshua Wilson also works at Monkpark, where he flies his birds of prey for visitor entertainment. He lives a lonely existence but he has reasons for choosing isolation – and, in Amy, he may have found somebody who understands.

Then a management change brings slick and well-spoken Edmund Evershott to Monkpark. He's interested in Amy too, but for what reason? Josh suspects the new manager is up to no good – but will Amy? Because Edmund could leave her with much worse than a broken heart …

Available in paperback from all good bookshops and online stores. Visit www.choc-lit.com for details.

The Girl on the Beach

Morton S. Gray

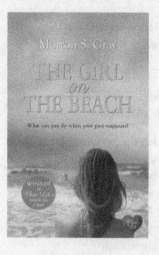

Who is Harry Dixon?

When Ellie Golden meets Harry Dixon, she can't help but feel she recognises him from somewhere. But when she finally realises who he is, she can't believe it – because the man she met on the beach all those years before wasn't called Harry Dixon. And, what's more, that man is dead.

For a woman trying to outrun her troubled past and protect her son, Harry's presence is deeply unsettling – and even more disconcerting than coming face to face with a dead man, is the fact that Harry seems to have no recollection of ever having met Ellie before. At least that's what he says …

But perhaps Harry isn't the person Ellie should be worried about. Because there's a far more dangerous figure from the past lurking just outside of the new life she has built for herself, biding his time, just waiting to strike.

Winner of Choc Lit's 2016 Search for a Star competition!

Available in paperback from all good bookshops and online stores. Visit www.choc-lit.com for details.

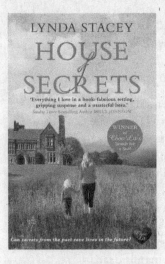

House of Secrets
Lynda Stacey

A woman on the run, a broken man and a house with a shocking secret ...

Madeleine Frost has to get away. Her partner Liam has become increasingly controlling to the point that Maddie fears for her safety, and that of her young daughter Poppy.

Desperation leads Maddie to the hotel owned by her estranged father – the extraordinarily beautiful Wrea Head Hall in Yorkshire. There, she meets Christopher 'Bandit' Lawless, an ex-marine and the gamekeeper of the hall, whose brusque manner conceals a painful past.

After discovering a diary belonging to a previous owner, Maddie and Bandit find themselves immersed in the history of the old house, uncovering its secrets, scandals, tragedies – and, all the while, becoming closer.

But Liam still won't let go, he wants Maddie back, and when Liam wants something he gets it, no matter who he hurts ...

Winner of Choc Lit's 2015 Search for a Star competition!

Available in paperback from all good bookshops and online stores. Visit www.choc-lit.com for details.

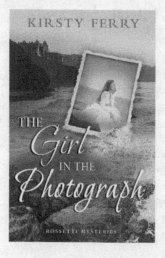

The Girl in the Photograph

Kirsty Ferry

What if the past was trying to teach you a lesson?

Staying alone in the shadow of an abandoned manor house in Yorkshire would be madness to some, but art enthusiast Lissy de Luca can't wait. Lissy has her reasons for seeking isolation, and she wants to study the Staithes Group – an artists' commune active at the turn of the twentieth century.

Lissy is fascinated by the imposing Sea Scarr Hall – but the deeper she delves, the stranger things get. A lonely figure patrols the cove at night, whilst a hidden painting leads to a chilling realisation. And then there's the photograph of the girl; so beautiful she could be a mermaid … and so familiar.

As Lissy further immerses herself, she comes to an eerie conclusion. The occupants of Sea Scarr Hall are long gone, but they have a message for her – and they're going to make sure she gets it.

Available in paperback from all good bookshops and online stores. Visit www.choc-lit.com for details.

Introducing Choc Lit